The Rider

Vancouver, BC, Canada

ISBN: 978-1-928196-21-1

The Rider

Also by Edward Mullen

The Art of the Hustle

The Art of the Hustle 2

Destiny and Free Will

Prodigy

Prodigy Eternal

Prodigy Returns

The Secret Manuscript

Eden

I am Rome

Zero

How this Story Came to Be

The story about how The Rider came to be is worth sharing since it's unique in my writing career. Ideas come and go and while riding bikes with my wife, I had this sudden flash of a scene in my head of a lone rider, racing through a mars-like terrain on a futuristic bike - abandoned buildings, sand covered roads, and a mysterious hint of danger. I thought the visual looked really cool and that it would make a great opening scene of a movie where you're unsure what's happening, who this rider is, what he looks like, where he's going, or what he's running from.

I caught up to my wife who always rides her bike a bit faster than me, and I described the imagery I had in my head. I said, "Wouldn't that be a cool scene in a movie?" I then asked, "If the movie opened with that scene, what would the rest of the movie be about?"

Without missing a beat, she went on to explain in great detail her concept of what would become The Rider. She came up with several key plot points, the backstory and reason why certain things happened, and she even came up with an ending.

Now, I should say, I have never seen my wife's creativity before, and had no idea she was even interested in talking about book or movie plots, but I feel like I found a secret weapon.

"Tell me more," I said.

For the next thirty minutes as we biked home, we volleyed ideas back and forth, becoming ever more enthused about this plot.

She said enthusiastically, "You have to write this story!"

I had to admit, it was a really good collaboration that was completely spontaneous. It has never happened before or since, but for that moment, we captured lighting in a bottle and she was in the zone.

When we got home, I wrote the opening chapter, which has pretty much remained the same as I wrote it that day. If you decide to read this story, you will read that scene next. It came out just the way I wanted it in the first draft. I also jotted down all the ideas we had come up with on that fateful bike ride so I wouldn't forget.

Over the next couple of days, more ideas came to us and we continued to build the plot. However, at the time, I was busy with a million other projects and life and I put it on the back burner with the hopes of eventually picking it up one day. But, I have countless first chapters and outlines on my computer and the reality is, I will likely never get around to writing any of them. But I didn't want that to happen to this idea because I felt like it was ours and that was somehow special.

One day, I moved some things around in my schedule to carve out time in my day to write. I found that my creative juices were flowing the most during the day while my brain was still fresh. At night, I usually just want to relax. So while at my day job, I would take 10 minutes to eat my lunch and then I would sneak off to a far corner of the office, sit in large cubical-style chair with my laptop on my lap, and aim to type at least a thousand words. Most days I would get to around 1500 – 2000, which I was very happy with. I would email the chapters to myself, then when I would get home, I would add them to the main story document like I was making deposits in a piggy bank.

I got about 75% of the story complete when I finally talked to Sky about where the story had evolved and developed into, because I was tasked with writing it, she was no longer involved in the project after that one day. So naturally as I write, the story takes twists and turns, and develops in ways that may deviate from our original concept.

She was disappointed that I didn't include a love story. I remember exactly where we were - we were on the UBC campus (University of British Columbia, which is where we both went to school but hadn't met yet), in the village to be exact. We had taken our dog Pipi out on a Sunday so that he could get some exercise and a change of scenery.

We argued about a love story and I gave her examples of successful movies and books that did not have a love story, but she persisted. In the end, I decided that I could go back and work in a love story.

The other thing she was adamant about (for some reason) was the ending, which I cannot tell you about. However, despite me being against her ideas about the love story and the ending, I decided to include both. So it only seemed right that I put her name on the cover with me. This is our story, we hope you like it.

This is our story, we hope you like it.

Chapter One

A desolate wasteland, a shattered civilization, a routine run — a lone rider raced through a deserted city, hoping to reach his destination before nightfall.

A thick and ever-present orange smog obstructed his view as he meandered through the empty streets of the once prosperous city. Bouncing around the rough terrain, the rider shifted his weight as he accelerated beyond 200 km/h. The bike hardly made a sound.

An unpiloted drone trailed behind as the rider cut through hollowed out buildings and tunnels, taking the shortest route possible to the drop point.

Flying a hundred feet above, the drone made its descent, getting closer to the rider. The high-pitched buzzing sound of the drone ricocheted off the sterile buildings like an echo chamber.

As it hovered directly above the bike, a flashing light appeared in the rider's helmet display, and a small compartment on the back of the bike automatically opened up, allowing the drone to dock and become stowed away.

The drone had been scanning the landscape the entire time and projecting the data in real-time. The heads-up display within his helmet kept him informed of his surroundings, an absolute lifeline on these sorts of missions. The temperature remained steady at 40 degrees Celsius. A west wind was picking up, impairing the already limited visibility. There were no signs of life anywhere. Oxygen levels – barely registered.

In the distance, the rider saw movement, which was unusual in these parts. The momentary distraction was enough to take his eyes off the road for a split second. Directly in front of him was an up-heaved slab of concrete that approached too fast for him to avoid. He attempted to swerve around the hazard, but the tires hit the lifted piece of road like a ramp, sending the bike airborne and slightly off kilter.

When the wheels touched down, the rider's balance was off, throwing him to one side of the bike. The bike's suspension compressed, which made regaining control even more challenging. Just up ahead was a low hanging obstacle in the middle of the road. The suspension recoiled at the same time the rider needed to duck underneath a fallen streetlamp. He quickly hunkered low on his bike, but it was not enough. The top of his helmet clipped the streetlamp, peeling him off the back. The bike ghost-rided for 30 to 40 feet before toppling over and skidding to a stop.

The rider lay motionless on his back with his eyes closed. He eventually awoke by the alarming sound that nobody ever wanted to hear — a signal that his oxygen was running low.

His eyes opened slowly and he rolled onto his side, wincing in pain. Struggling to regain consciousness, he ignored the warning. He never travelled with anything less than a full day's worth of oxygen so he figured the alarm must be a glitch.

The rider, dressed in all black armour, returned to his feet unscathed from the crash. With a scattered brain, he pulled himself together — first ensuring he had no broken bones, then checking his equipment for damage — two things he could not afford to go wrong in these parts. Next, he checked the time and realized he had been unconscious for a little over a minute.

He knew these roads all too well, but the roadblock was new. Perhaps it was placed there on purpose — a trap for unsuspecting travellers. The rider withdrew his gun and cautiously walked back to his bike. Being so exposed made him nervous. There were known and unknown evils lurking in these parts, and there were just too many places to hide for him to feel safe. With a stiff neck and a slight limp, he scanned the immediate area for any threats.

The alarm once again blared with urgency, demanding his immediate attention. "Oxygen levels low," a robotic female voice permeated throughout his helmet. "Restock your oxygen levels. Less than one hour remaining."

Taking a deep breath, the rider removed the oxygen canister from his helmet and noticed it had been damaged in the crash. Nearly a day's worth of the precious liquid oxygen had spilled out and become absorbed by the porous road.

He quickly replaced the canister and exhaled before taking another breath. With only an hour supply of oxygen and being more than an hour from his destination, time was of the essence. He made a small adjustment to his helmet to restrict the airflow and walked briskly back to his bike, ensuring he kept his heart rate low. With a little luck, he may just make it, but it would be cutting it close. Nevertheless, limiting his oxygen intake only added to his already throbbing head.

Typically a rider only travelled with one canister, taking any more was just asking for trouble. There were just too many bandits and dangers along the way so they didn't want to make themselves unnecessary targets. With one full canister costing more than most people can afford in a month, it was imperative to just take what one needed.

Picking his bike off the ground, several forms were identified in his helmet. Two hiding up ahead, two more sneaking up behind him, and at least one more in an adjacent building.

The rider calmly mounted his bike and deployed the drone. The back hatch of the bike opened up and the drone rocketed skyward, blasting out several smoke grenades. The exploding canisters created the perfect smoke screen, encompassing the bike in all directions. Not even the most advanced sensors could penetrate through the dense cloud.

The rider took off, punching through the smoke like a stealth panther not making a sound. Abandoned cars, broken down and rusted, littered the congested streets, but the rider knew the way. He had travelled this route a thousand times. With limited visibility, he relied on his experience, swerving in and out of the hazard-filled roads toward the city limits. From there, was nothing but straight highway.

The hazy sun slowly retreated turning the sky from a dark butterscotch to black. The moon and stars hadn't been visible in decades.

A persistent flashing light in the upper corner indicated his oxygen level, which was dropping rapidly. The temporary adrenaline dump demanded more oxygen than he had to spare, so he tried his best to control his breathing. He was not sure who or what was trying to get him back there, but he was happy that was behind him. He had a delivery to make and more importantly, he needed to save his own life. He couldn't afford any more setbacks.

"Oxygen levels low," the voice spoke again. "You have less than one minute remaining."

Heavy on the throttle, the bike reached top speed and charged into the city like a streak of light. Battling through a severe concussion and sipping oxygen for the past hour, the rider was on the verge of passing out at any second. His body desperately craved the life-dependent element as several parts of his body tingled and went numb.

With the drop point in sight, the rider pulled up to the facility in the nick of time. A coughing fit nearly incapacitated him as he gasped for breath. Dismounting his bike, the biometric scan at the entrance of the building granted him access. Collapsing to the floor, the rider pulled off his helmet just before he completely suffocated. He inhaled a deep breath, and then another. The facility's oxygen, the cheap synthetic kind that would give a person a headache, filled his lungs and kept him alive.

Chapter Two

Laying on the ground, the rider took a few seconds to recuperate. Oxy-freeloaders, as they were known, were frowned upon and security was quick to escort him off the premises where he would surely die.

"Okay, pal, let's go. Get up. You have to leave," one of guards said.

"I have... a package," the rider muttered.

"What's that?"

"Delivery," the rider said. "I have a delivery."

"You have a delivery? For who?"

"The boss," the rider said, flashing a digital badge with his nearly limp arm.

The guards' attitudes completely changed as they helped the rider to his feet. "Our sincerest apologies, sir. Can we get you anything to eat or drink?"

"I just want to deliver my package and go."

"Sure thing. Right this way, sir."

As the synthetic oxygen entered the rider's bloodstream, it gave him a second wind. Within minutes, he felt much better.

Two security guards escorted the rider down a long corridor toward a private elevator in which they all entered and rode to the top floor. When the doors opened, the rider looked at the guards as he walked passed them.

"Kade Casey, you're late," Mr. Saigon said. "Where the hell have you been?"

"It's funny you mention hell," Kade said. "Let's just say I experienced a minor setback, but... I'm here... with your package, as usual."

Kade stepped forward and handed over a small package with undisclosed contents. Mr. Saigon accepted the package and looked at the rider's scuffed-up helmet and dented canister, but didn't ask any further questions. All he cared about was his package.

The rider had clients all over the city, but Mr. Saigon was known to pay the best. Kade never knew what he was transporting and never cared, as long as he received payment.

Upon handing over the package, Mr. Saigon gave the rider payment — a single canister of pure liquid oxygen, enough to last an entire month if rationed correctly.

"Thanks," Kade said, swapping out the damaged canister for the new one and placing his helmet back on his head. Kade kept his interaction to a minimum. He turned away and walked toward the guards who were still waiting by the elevator.

Kade left Mr. Saigon's office and rode through town. He pulled into the underground parking garage in his building, parked his bike, and made his way to the ground floor. There was a 24 hour sushi spot on the same block that he ate at regularly when he would come home late and didn't want to cook.

On his way to the restaurant, various digital stats displayed on the visor of his helmet — an advertisement for a local watering hole, a biometric breakdown of some pedestrians walking by, the time, weather forecast, temperature, and oxygen levels — below 5%. The streets were empty except for the broken down cars and piles of garbage that littered the sides of the streets. The only good thing about living in a dump was there were no rodents, even they could not survive with such low levels of oxygen.

In the distance was Megalopolis, a towering city of modern architecture and bright lights — one of only a handful of cities remaining in the world. Population — less than a million.

Amid the sleazy remnants of a once prosperous neighbourhood was an equally rundown hole in the wall that stood for a sushi restaurant. It should be illegal to call what they served as sushi, but it was sustenance nevertheless. When Kade entered the late-night establishment, a notification was sent to him, visible on his visor. Kade reached out and touched the augmented reality app, which expanded into a large menu.

"Welcome to Sushi Mura," a digital woman greeted him, "What would you like?"

Without saying a word, Kade swiped through the choices on the virtual screen and selected a few items. For payment, he selected the 'Pay' icon and the money was automatically withdrawn from his account and transferred to the restaurant. Six units for a bento box was considered cheap, but then again, there was not a lot of customers coming in this late at night.

Units were the official global currency, but for larger transactions, merchants and others would often accept oxygen as payment as well.

Kade took a seat at a table in one of the corners. In his helmet, he could connect to his messages, media accounts, news, and entertainment. He briefly scrolled through a list of news articles, catching up on anything he missed throughout the day.

Just then an invitation to speak came up on his screen. A short video loop of his friend came up. He tapped the side of his helmet to minimize everything in his display and then retracted the visor on his helmet. He was now looking at his friend face to face.

"Kade, what's good, my guy?"

"Tanjoban, it's good to see you. What are you doing out so late?"

"I could ask you the same thing."

"Just got back from a job."

"Oh yeah, same. How did yours go?"

"It was... eventful. I took a nasty spill and was nearly attacked by rogues."

"Are you being serious? You're the best rider I know, how the hell did you wipe out?"

"I think I fell into a trap. I've made that trip a thousand times and can practically do it in my sleep. There's a part of the road that was raised up like a jump and I hit it going over 100 km/h. I caught a little airtime, but up ahead was a downed streetlight. I tried to duck under it, but the top of my helmet clipped it. It nearly took my head clean off.

"There were rogues all around me. I counted at least five. I got back on my bike and booked it out of there as fast as I could.

"Good thing. Who knows what those savages would have done to me."

"That's crazy. I had something similar happen to me once," Tanjoban said.

"Fortunately I made it out alive... this time. I have a killer headache, but otherwise I'm fine. I nearly drained though. My canister was damaged in the crash and most of my oxygen leaked out."

"Sounds like a real adventure. I haven't had one of those in a while."

"Yeah, I'm just glad to be back in my bed tonight. Live to ride another day."

"That's what it's all about."

"Well, I'm not sure what it's all about, but maybe I'll figure it out tomorrow."

Kade's order came up so he grabbed his food, said goodbye to his friend, and went back to him apartment. On his way home, a prostitute passed him by and sent him an invitation for a late-night rendezvous. The request came up on his heads-up display, displaying a short looped video of her face and body without the mask. Kade tapped the side of his helmet to ignore the invitation, set his privacy to unavailable, and kept walking.

Kade didn't want to take the stairs, but the elevator had been out for the past several months. His apartment building was pretty quiet aside from his neighbour, who always played his VR too loud. Kade placed his hand on a sensor and the door unlocked and slid open.

Waiting for him in the front entrance of his apartment was his dog Digi — a miniature robot dog that did not require food, walking, and most importantly, oxygen. Kade greeted his dog affectionately as if it were a living animal.

"Heya, boy, did you miss me?" he said, bending down to comfort the electronic dog. "Who's a good boy?"

The dog showed him positive signs of affection and followed him faithfully into the kitchen where Kade set his food down on the counter.

The apartment was air sealed and maintained a livable amount of oxygen at all times. Using a digital panel mounted on the wall, he adjusted the levels so that he could get a little more comfortable. Since leaving Mr. Saigon's office, he had been breathing pure oxygen, which had enriched his blood. It didn't take long for his body to recharge.

Kade removed his helmet, jacket, and boots before entering his bedroom and placing his hand on a part of the wall. A secret panel opened up containing all his valuable oxygen that he had been saving, nearly six months' worth. He removed the canisters that he had received for his latest delivery and placed them with the others. With a simple touch, the secret wall panel sealed back up and locked into place.

After each delivery, Kade usually soaked his air filters, but he decided he'd do that in the morning. He wanted to take some time off and not take on any new deliveries, so there was no rush.

Taking his food into the living room, Kade sat in front of the TV, eating his meal and catching a moment of much needed rest.

Taking his food into the living room, Kade sat in front of the TV, eating his meal and catching a moment of much needed rest.

Chapter Three

With his status set to unavailable, Kade was unreachable. He was not taking any new jobs for the immediate future.

He left his apartment building around noon to run some errands. One of the things on his to do list was to visit his mother. She was sick and unable to work so Kade delivered groceries and other essentials to her every other day. As the world was consumed by a thick smog that choked the life out of nearly every living thing, those who survived often developed life-threatening respiratory ailments. His mother required constant care and Kade made it his life's mission to look after her. In many ways, her life gave him purpose — a reason to continue. Living in a world so bleak had a way of robbing people of joy and hope.

Kade entered his mother's apartment, greeted her with a hug, and then set two canisters of oxygen on the counter for her.

"How're you feeling?" he asked. "Can I get you anything? Something to eat?"

"I just made myself a sandwich. I made one for you as well. It's in the fridge."

"Thanks."

"Where are you off to next?" his mother asked. "Another job?"

"I don't plan on taking any more jobs for a little while. I just want to stay in the city and be close to you."

"I'd really enjoy that, Kaden. You know I worry about you so much. Not a day goes by where I don't pray for you to come home safe and sound."

"There's no reason to pray, mum. If there is a God, he's not answering his calls," Kade said, walking to the air purifying system. He replaced his mother's air filter and put in a new oxygen canister.

"As long as we're still alive and breathing, God is looking out for us," his mother said.

"I hope you're right about that."

Kade sat next to his mum on the couch and pulled a token out of his pocket. "Before coming to see you, I had a meeting. Look," he said, showing his mother a one-year sobriety coin. "I'm one year clean today."

"That's so wonderful, honey. Come here," his mother said, hugging him and shedding a tear. "I'm so proud of you."

"We should celebrate," Kade said. "Where would you like to go?"

"Dinner and a movie?"

"It's a date."

Kade spent the afternoon with his mother, and at around 6:00 p.m., the two exited the building. The city was dark and they lived in a rough part of town.

"I never leave the house this late," Kade's mother said.

"It's okay, ma, you're safe with me."

The streets were seedy. Nefarious and opportunistic criminals lurked in the shadows, looking for an easy target. Most of them were addicted to ghost, the street name for a synthetic drug that when inhaled delivered a power psychedelic experience of euphoria. The drug was widespread through the area, everyone trying to get their hands on it. It was nearly as valuable as oxygen.

"You know, this reminds me of a much more innocent time," she said. "Before the volcano, people went to work, went out on dates, met with friends, ran their daily errands... So much has changed. I hardly know any of my neighbours, most people work from home, and rarely do they go out and meet up with friends in person. Wherever I look I see unscrupulous characters littered all over, doing drugs and up to no good. It's a really sad state."

"I try not to think about it. This is the world I know. I was just a little kid when the volcano erupted."

"I wish you could have seen the way people lived back in the day."

"There's always videos online. I get the idea."

"It's not the same."

They continued down the dark streets, illuminated by the soft glow from the streetlights, Kade's mother clung to his arm. Her anxiety was spiked and she didn't feel comfortable being out at night.

While crossing a street, they heard a commotion in a back alley that sounded like a woman screaming. She was crying for help and fighting off her attacker. Kade continued walking, paying her no mind.

"Kaden, you must help that poor woman."

"It's best not to get involved, ma," he said, not breaking stride.

"That is someone's sister, or mother. You must help her."

"We live it a different world now, ma. If I help her, I might get jumped, stabbed, or shot. Is that what you want?"

"Of course not, but we can't turn a blind eye," his mother said, stopping dead in her tracks.

"Ma, what are you doing? It's most likely a trap. People out here are hustlers. They trick you into thinking there's danger, and when you go to help, five guys will surround you and rob you. Trust me, it's best not to get involved."

"I didn't raise you to be a coward. Now either you go help her, or I will."

Kade looked at his mother and realized she wasn't budging until he did something. Too often people, including Kade, would turn a blind eye to these sorts of situations, which were a regular occurrence. Rapes, murders, muggings, anyone in distress were left to their own devices. The problems were easier to ignore than to acknowledge. It was common for people to step over a dead body like a piece of discarded trash and carry on with their day without giving second thought. It was a harsh environment and human life, aside from one's own, just wasn't seen as valuable.

Withdrawing his gun, he entered the alley, charging into the darkness. He called out to the woman, whose screams had now subsided. Her attackers had fled. Approaching the woman, Kade was still cautious, looking around for a potential ambush. Still brandishing his weapon, he asked the woman if she was okay.

The young girl, no more than fifteen years old, was slumped over and sobbing uncontrollably. She looked up at Kade, but didn't share her profile with him so he had no way of telling what she looked like or how old she was. He at least could tell that she was emotionally distraught and in need of help.

"It's okay, I won't hurt you," he said, discreetly tucking the gun into his jacket. He then extended a hand to help her up. Kade helped the poor girl to her feet and escorted her back to the main street, where Kade's mother was waiting with open arms.

"My name is Kade, what's your name?"

"My name is, Kirin," the girl said.

"It's nice to meet you, Kirin. We're here to help you. Is there somewhere you'd like to go? My mother and I can walk with you to make sure you get there safely."

"A young girl like you shouldn't be out on these streets alone," Kade's mother said. "It's not safe."

"I appreciate your help and concern, but I should go."

"Are you sure?" Kade's mother said. "Let us walk you home at least."

"No, really, I'm fine. Thank you," the girl said before darting across the street in a hurry.

"What has this world come to?" his mother said.

"People are just reverting to their animalistic tendencies. There are hunters, and there are prey."

"I don't believe that," his mother shot back. "What are you? What am I?"

"We're prey. We're just not the weakest targets yet."

"This poor girl shouldn't have been out at night. These streets aren't safe."

"It's a concrete jungle, ma," Kade said, reflecting on the situation. "Survival of the fittest out here."

Chapter Four

It had only been a couple of days since Kade made his last delivery with Saigon. Two in a month was the norm – two in one week was a gift. Everyone in town knew Saigon's reputation for paying the best, but that wasn't the reputation Kade was thinking about. Saigon was also known as a ruthless scoundrel who used forceful, and even deadly, tactics to get what he wanted. He was not a man one wanted to be on his bad side, and refusing a job was the surest way to get there.

Kade was in the middle of repairing his drone when he received an incoming message. He decided to ignore it and return to his work. Less than twenty minutes later, another message came in. This time, Kade checked. They were both from Mr. Saigon — he was requesting Kade's services. Even though Kade had his delivery status set to unavailable, the messages were marked as urgent.

Kade read the message and thought for a moment how he should respond. Letting out an exaggerated sigh, Kade wrote, "Mr. Saigon, I appreciate the request, but I'm not making any more deliveries until next week. Equipment repairs."

Seconds later, Mr. Saigon replied. "Send me your location, I will have someone pick you up. This matter is of the upmost importance."

Mr. Saigon was not one to take no for an answer. Refusal to meet Mr. Saigon could cause him to go off the rails and do something irrational. He was unpredictable. Kade felt it would be best to comply with the request so he sent a ping to Mr. Saigon, which showed his real-time coordinates. On the other end, Saigon was staring at a digital map waiting for the signal. Once it came up, he sent his driver to retrieve Kade.

Kade messaged his friend Tanjoban to see if he had any experience with Mr. Saigon such as this. Tanjoban hadn't had the experience, nor had he heard of it happening to any of the other riders. This wasn't business as usual.

The entire time Kade was working, his mind was preoccupied with what it could possibly be. It was making him anxious. Kade made a point of never inquiring about or inspecting the contents of his deliveries. He mostly assumed it was spice, drugs, or some other banal object of desire from one elite to another. He wondered what could possibly be so important that demanded such urgency.

A car service pulled up to Kade's building and alerted him. Kade peered out the window and saw an all-black SUV and what appeared to be a single driver.

"Be back in a bit," Kade said to his dog, Digi. He grabbed his helmet from the kitchen counter and shoved it on his head. The digital display lit up, he had plenty of oxygen to last him the rest of the week. "Protect the castle in my absence," he said, walking toward the front door of his apartment.

The dog made an artificial bark sound before following him faithfully to the door.

"Digi, track my location. If I don't return within the hour, send help."

Kade made his way down several flights of stairs before stepping outside. A proximity sensor alerted the driver. They exchanged a formal greeting before Kade was invited into the backseat. Not a word was spoken between him and the driver the entire way.

The vehicle drove through the rundown part of town where Kade lived into the nice part of town to where Saigon lived. Saigon was the richest man in the city and fittingly lived in the tallest tower. On a clear day, the tower could be visible from any point in the city, but there were never any clear days.

As the vehicle pulled into the underground parking facility, Kade's nervous energy grew stronger. Mr. Saigon was not one to mess with, and without any indication of what he wanted, Kade's imagination ran wild with all kinds of unpleasant scenarios.

The driver got out first and opened the passenger door so that Kade could exit the vehicle. "This way," he said, instructing Kade to follow him. Kade walked closely behind as they entered the building, walked down a hallway, and entered into an elevator. Kade opted to remove his helmet even though the oxygen he was breathing was a higher grade than that artificial junk Mr. Saigon pumped throughout his building. Anytime he could preserve his precious oxygen, he opted for that.

The elevator raced to the top floor and Kade and Mr. Saigon's driver stood next to each other in silence. When they reached the top floor, the doors of the private elevator split open and Kade stepped out by himself. The doors closed behind him and he could hear the elevator go back down. This added to his nerves. He was without his bike and weapons, and felt a little vulnerable. Nevertheless, if Mr. Saigon wanted to hurt him, he wouldn't bring him to his office.

"Kade Casey, good to see you," Mr. Saigon said. The towering man was impeccably dressed as usual. There was a slender woman with him with slick black hair and a form-fitting black dress – Veronica James – Kade had met her before.

"What can I do for you, boss?" Kade asked, glad-handing the high-roller.

"I have a job for you."

"Another delivery?" Kade asked.

"Yes. Please, have a seat."

Kade sat in an oversized chair, which made him feel even more insignificant in Saigon's presence. He wondered if Saigon did this intentionally to invoke such feelings of insecurity and give him an advantage in his business dealings.

"Tri-City," Saigon said. That's all he needed to say. Kade could fill in the rest.

"Sorry, I don't make deliveries that far East."

Mr. Saigon chuckled a bit, flashing his sinister smile. He picked up a large object from his desk and for a second, Kade thought he was going to fling it at his head or beat him to death with it. Without saying a word, Mr. Saigon walked over to a bottle of whiskey and poured himself a glass.

"Whiskey?" he offered.

"No, thank you."

"I'm sorry, where are my manners," Mr. Saigon said in an insincere tone. "I understand you've had a bit of a substance issue in the past."

'How the hell did he know that?' Kade thought. His nerves came flaring back as he swallowed hard and began to sweat. He wondered what Mr. Saigon was insinuating. Every word Mr. Saigon spoke was calculated and said for a particular reason. Kade attempted to anticipate where he was going with that remark. Mr. Saigon's theatrical antics made him even more threatening as one really wasn't sure what exactly he was thinking.

"Don't worry about it," Kade said.

"Now, Mr. Casey. Suppose I wanted a package delivered to Tri-City, and I wanted to hire the best rider in town. Who would I call?"

It was a leading question and Kade knew it.

"I supposed you'd call me, sir," Kade said nervously.

"Perfect, then I've made the right call. Now, if you were me, and you were talking to the best rider in town, and this rider refused to deliver a package. What do you think would be the appropriate response?"

"I...I'm not sure."

Mr. Saigon got up and walked over to him with a slow and methodical pace. He then circled around the back of the chair Kade was in. Kade was expecting some sort of blow to come his way and braced for impact. "Relax," Mr. Saigon said. "You seem tense."

"Just ah... been a stressful week," Kade replied.

"I can imagine. How's your mother doing?"

Now this was definitely a shot fired. 'How does Saigon know about my mother?'

"My mother?" Kade asked.

"She's doing alright I presume?"

This comment lit a fire under Kade. His heart started to race and his blood began to boil. He wasn't exactly sure what to do with all that energy. It wasn't as though he was going to get up and fight Mr. Saigon, and he could not just leave – so neither fight or flight were viable options. Saigon had a larger than life stature. He was nearly a foot taller than Kade and outweighed him by more than a hundred pounds. Kade felt as though he was trapped inside a cage with a grizzly bear.

"I'm not sure what to tell you," Kade said, trying to sound confident. "You need a package delivered to Tri-City and I don't go to Tri-City, so..."

"Anyone can go anywhere, it's a matter of will."

"It's too dangerous. Whatever reward you are offering is not worth the risk. I'm sure there there are plenty of other riders–"

"I DON'T WANT ANY OTHER RIDER!" Saigon shouted, slamming his fist down on his desk.

"Look, Mr. Saigon, with all due respect, what matters to you is having your package delivered, right? And I would love to be that guy for you, but I don't know those routes, I don't have relationships along the way, and you really need both if you plan to make it there an back in one piece. I just don't think I'm the best guy. Now, if you want me to go to Hive, Ashen, or Tribeca then I'm your guy. But Tri-City, I'm sorry, but you're going to have to find someone else."

"But you're the best rider in the city. Isn't that what you said?"

"Look, if you don't mind, I have some work I need to return to and some places I need to be. If I'm late, people are going to be concerned and come looking for me."

"Of course, I would hate to cause anyone concern."

Kade took it as another passive aggressive remark, but didn't react. He walked toward the elevator and pressed the button.

"Six canisters," Mr. Saigon said in his stoic voice.

This was the largest offer he had ever received and it definitely made him stop dead in his tracks. Most riders would jump at the chance to earn just one canister. Kade turned around slowly. Saigon smiled then looked at him with his usual no-nonsense demeanour.

"That's a very generous offer, but like I said, I need to be somewhere, I need to rest up, and possibly reevaluate my life choices."

"Eight canisters."

By now Kade was already in the elevator, he pressed the button to the lobby several times hoping it would make the doors close faster. He wanted to get out of there as quickly as possible. He looked up and saw Mr. Saigon was now standing in the doorway, preventing the doors from shutting.

"Ten. You'll receive half payment upfront, and the rest upon successful delivery."

"Not for nothing, I appreciate the offer, really, but it's a fool's errand. See, I don't get paid when I deliver the package, I get paid when I come back, which is twice the risk. You on the other hand, have your package delivered with one trip, but I only get paid after making two trips. So the odds of you having your package delivered and not having to pay me are considerably higher. And we both know the risks involved going to Tri-City. So like I said, with all due respect, I will have to decline you offer."

Kade thought he might die in that elevator, but to his surprise, Mr. Saigon stepped back allowing the doors to close.

"I'm disappointed, Kade, and I hope you reconsider my offer," Mr. Saigon said as the elevator doors closed. Mr. Saigon then said one final thing that sent chills down his spine. "Say hello to your mother for me."

The elevator took him to the bottom floor and when he stepped out, there was a wall of Mr. Saigon's goons waiting for him. They were dressed in black, but did not look like they were going to a formal event. Kade thought for sure he was in for a long night.

Kade stepped out of the elevator and the goons surrounded him. He was trapped with nowhere to run. He thought about reconsidering his position, but would rather take a beating that he would likely survive than a trip that he likely wouldn't. With his head high, Kade march confidently toward the group of men.

Much to his surprise, the men stepped aside, allowing Kade to exit. It was an intimidation tactic, that's all. Once outside, Kade couldn't believe he had made it out of Mr. Saigon's building unscathed, although he knew this was far from over.

Chapter Five

Kade stood on the opposite side of the street from a little coffee shop called Chu's Wisely, a local gathering for misfits and downtrodden souls who frequented the Collingwood district. The owner, Mr. Chu, was a well-respected business man who was a former agent for Mr. Saigon and the Ho Chi Minh gang. He was somewhat of a legend in the neighbourhood ever since he branched out on his own, using his power and influence for good, to help those in need and offer them protection.

Kade looked both ways before cutting across the street, disappearing into the shop. In addition to the food and beverage items a customer bought, they were also charged an oxygen fee for each minute they were inside, which of course was sold at a premium. That's how a lot of these small businesses made their money. Most places offered cheap synthetic air, which was comprised of mostly nitrogen and only trace amounts of recycled oxygen that had been processed through nasty filters.

Upon scanning in, Kade was permitted access. He found Tanjoban sitting inconspicuously in the back wearing a shirt that said 'Powerful JRE'. Kade walked over to him, sat down, and removed his helmet.

"I'm screwed," Kade said in a muted tone.

"Why, what's up?"

Tanjoban was a rider just like Kade. They ran in a small circle of riders who delivered packages, mostly for wealthy business owners and other social elites. The gig paid well, but it was not without its dangers.

"I've been offered a job," Kade said.

"How much are they paying?"

"Ten canisters."

"Saigon?"

"Yeah."

"Let me guess, Tri-City?"

Kade nodded before looking over his shoulder. It was a new habit he had picked up and hadn't stopped ever since leaving Mr. Saigon's office.

"Please tell me you declined."

"You know how Saigon is," Kade said. "Can you really decline?"

"So what happened? I want to know everything."

"Ever since my trip back from Hive, I had my status set to unavailable. I needed a few days off. I was really looking forward to relaxing and spending time with my mum."

"How's she doing by the way?"

"She's doing fine, but I worry about her. I'm not sure how much time she has left, so the time I spend with her is important. But not only that, when I'm gone, she doesn't have anyone to look after her. I think about that on some of these jobs, you know? If I were to die or... I don't know, something bad were to happen to me where I'm gone for a really long time, then... I don't know, maybe I should just do something else with my life, something with fewer occupational hazards."

"Yeah, I'm sure you'll figure it out. Go back to your story, tell me everything that happened with you and Saigon."

"I was at home, fixing my equipment, and Saigon kept blowing me up. It was one message after the other. I tried to ignore him, but that didn't seem like the right thing to do. Eventually, I had to answer, you know? He says he has a job for me and insists we meet. He asks for my location and the next thing I know, there's a car service in front of my building, waiting to take me to his tower. I meet the driver outside, but he barely says a word. The whole time I'm thinking something seems off about this whole situation. So the driver takes me to his office, and with each passing

second, I'm growing more nervous. I have this pit in my
stomach where I feel like I want to throw up. I contemplated
having the driver pull over and just run away, disappear
into the city and lay low."

"It was probably good thing that you didn't do that. You
know Saigon, he has eyes and ears everywhere. You can't
really hide from him."

"Yeah. So any way, I feel like a lamb being led to the
slaughter. I arrive at his building and you know how it is, it's
intimidating. I feel like everything is designed to make me
feel small and unimportant."

"To him, you are."

"Yeah, well. I feel like I'm about to be a huge thorn in his
side."

"So what happened next?"

"I ride the elevator up to his office where he proceeds to
offer me this impossible job. But it's like this weird
doublespeak, you know? If you wrote down what he said, it
wouldn't seem like anything, but it was the way he said it,
you know? That insincere, sociopathic tone mixed with that
slow methodical swagger of a silver-back gorilla."

"I feel like he's unpredictable," Tanjoban remarked. "Do you
get that same impression?"

"Oh totally!"

"It's like he could fly off the rails at any moment and drive a dagger through your chest."

"Or more likely, your back," Kade said with a slight laugh. "I vividly recall having that exact thought."

"Okay, so what happened next?"

"I kept refusing his offer, throwing every excuse I had at this guy — my bike is in the shop, I need to reevaluate my life choices, I have to take care of my dog."

"Your dog takes care of himself."

"I know that, but he doesn't know that."

"Are you sure?"

"Actually, I forgot to mention until you just reminded me. He was saying all this weird stuff to me."

"Like what?"

"I don't know, like these passive aggressive threats. He was asking how my mother is doing and stuff like that. Actually, the very last thing he said to me before the elevator doors closed was, 'Say hi to your mother for me?'"

"'Say hi to your mother for me'? What the hell is that supposed to mean? Does he have a thing for your mother or something? I mean, Ms. Casey is fine and all, but—"

"Shut up, man."

"I'm just playing."

"Here's the thing," Kade said. "I don't think I ever mentioned my mother to him. He also knew I used to have a substance problem. He brought that up as well. It was a real game of chess in there."

"So he knows about your mum and your AA meetings, so what? For a guy like that, that doesn't surprise me. They say knowledge is power so I'm sure he has entire files on you... all of us. If we ever double cross him, he knows exactly where we live, what our weaknesses are, and what we value most."

"Yeah, maybe you're right, but it still doesn't change the fact that I refused his offer."

"I wouldn't worry too much about it. I'm sure he's calling some other rider to take the job as we speak. With a price of ten canisters, some schmuck is bound to take the job."

"I get the feeling whether I like it or not, I'm going to be that schmuck. Seriously, I don't know what to do, man," Kade said, burying his face in his palms.

"At the moment, you don't need to do anything," Tanjoban replied, trying to comfort his friend. "This could all be in your head. Sure, you probably soured your relationship with Saigon, but I'm sure he's already moved on to some other issue and isn't even thinking about you."

"You really think that?"

"Yeah, I wouldn't worry too much about it."

"So what should I do?"

"You said you plan to take some time off? Do that. You have enough 'O' to last you a while, so you're good, right?"

"Yeah."

"Okay, so relax, spend some time with your mum, take her out on a date so-to-speak."

"I have a hard time shutting my brain off. I know I'm going to obsess about this until I drive myself crazy."

"Whatever you do, don't go back to using ghost. We're in this recovery together, remember that."

"Don't worry, I've passed the year mark of being sober. I won't do anything to mess that up."

Tanjoban could see that his friend was hurting and wanted to offer him some sage advice, or do something to help out. He leaned in closer and lowered his voice. "Hey," he said, causing Kade to look up. "You know Mr. Chu may be able to help."

"How?" Kade replied in the same hushed tone.

"As you know, he's well connected, he used to work for Saigon. Maybe there's something he can do. We should go

have a chat with him. I'm sure he'll tell you that you have
nothing to worry about."

Chapter Six

Kade had met Mr. Chu a few times, but wasn't sure if Mr. Chu would remember him. The local business man interacted with a lot of people. Tanjoban on the other hand had done a few jobs for Chu and was on good terms with him.

"Stay here," Tanjoban said, standing up and walking to the back.

A moment later, Tanjoban emerged from behind a thick door and waved Kade to follow him. Kade stood up and looked around nervously before heading into the back of the coffee shop. Together, they walked down a long and narrow hallway until they approached another thick door. Tanjoban pounded on it and looked up at the security camera.

Proximity sensors scanned them and sent the information to whoever was on the other side of the door. Seconds later, a green light appeared on a panel by the door followed by a clicking sound. Tanjoban pushed open the heavy door and made his way to the centre of a small room.

The entire back wall was one giant high-res digital display that an artificial view of a jungle. The image was so clear, it looked like they had entered through a portal into the Congo.

"Mr. Chu," Tanjoban said, "This is my friend, Kade."

Mr. Chu stood up from behind his desk and walked over to greet Kade. In a coarse voice he spoke. "I believe we've met once or twice before if I'm not mistaken. Or perhaps I've seen you in passing."

"Yes, you are correct, sir. Thank you so much for meeting with me today, especially on such short notice."

"I always welcome company," Mr. Chu said with smile. "What can I do for you gentlemen?"

"Kade needs your help," Tanjoban said.

"Perhaps more advice than help," Kade corrected.

"Please, come and have a seat."

Kade looked at Tanjoban who gave him a reassuring nod. They both took their seats and were offered coffee.

"No, thank you. We had some earlier," Tanjoban said.

"Very well then. How can I be of assistance?"

"I've been given an offer for which I see no plausible reason to accept. I've rejected the offer, but now I fear the consequences for me will be worse than had I accepted."

"May I guess this offer is from Saigon?"

"Yes, sir."

"Can you tell me more about this offer?"

"He wants me to go to Tri-City to deliver a package."

"I see. And how much is the compensation?"

"Ten canisters."

Mr. Chu nodded as if he understood more than he was letting on. "And you refused this offer because making the trip is dangerous?"

"Correct."

"And since refusing, you fear your life may now be in danger?"

"Yes, sir."

"I believe I understand your predicament," he said like an old wise man.

"Is there anything I can do?" Kade asked.

Mr. Chu exhaled and spun around in his chair to gaze out at the fake view that was in front of him. Kade looked over at Tanjoban who gave him another nod of reassurance.

"This is my favourite part of the loop," Mr. Chu said. "Everyday around this time, the monkeys come out and play. It amuses me every time," he said with a chuckle.

Kade sat patiently, giving Mr. Chu the benefit of the doubt. It occurred to him that perhaps old age was starting to catch up with Mr. Chu and he was losing his mind.

After watching the monkeys descend from their digital trees and roll around in the tall grass, Mr. Chu spun his chair back around and was ready to deliver his King-Solomon-esque wisdom.

"Understanding the precise predicament you are in, I have given it some careful thought. Perhaps with more time and deliberation, I would arrive at a different conclusion entirely."

There was a pause.

"You are a delivery driver, correct?"

"Yes."

"This is how you make a living?"

"Yes, sir."

"You enjoy this line of work?"

"It's all I know."

"And Mr. Saigon is one of your main employers?"

"Yes."

"It seems to me you have three options — two of which are not advised. Your first option is to run and hide. This may sound simple, but I assure you, in such a world in which we live, it makes this option extremely difficult. Your digital footprint will alert anyone motivated enough to find you of your exact location the moment you step outside your door.

"You could of course move to another city, one that Saigon doesn't have a stronghold over, but in a twist of irony, the only city I know worth living is the one place for which you refuse to travel.

"Continuing with this thought, there's also the question of employment. By cutting off your main source of income, in this case life-supplying oxygen, you would need to find some other means of providing for yourself. But, you seem like a smart guy, I'm sure you find land on your feet with whatever you choose.

"Nevertheless, I think you will agree that this option is not an acceptable choice given the situation."

"I agree."

"Now, option two I'm afraid offers an equally unfavourable outcome. This is the choice that you have currently made —

refuse the offer and go about your daily life as if nothing has changed. I can assure you, Mr. Saigon is among the most petty of men and will do everything in his considerable power to destroy you. In the history of his rise to power, there has only been one man to successfully defy Saigon and live to tell about it. And that man is sitting in front of you."

"How did you do it?" Kade asked.

"It's a story for another time," Mr. Chu responded. "The short version is, you must have a considerable army, which I don't suspect you have."

"No, sir. My army is sitting beside me."

"Very well, as I had suspected. That leaves us with the third, and final option."

"Which is?"

"You make the delivery."

"I was afraid you would say that," Kade said, sinking lower into his chair like he had been deflated.

"What's your biggest concern about making the trip?" Mr. Chu asked. "Often the fear of something is greater than the reality."

"My biggest concern? I can think of about a dozen."

"Let's start with your biggest."

"Okay, let's see..." Kade said, taking his time. "There are transports that make that journey, but they travel in packs and are heavily armoured and weaponized. If I were to go, there's a limit to what I can carry."

"So your biggest concern is your load capacity?"

"Sorry, no... I was just..."

"Take your time."

"My concern is that I will be a team of one, which will not be enough to defend myself from an attack."

"Okay, so any given day, you could potentially get killed by any number of things, would you agree?"

"I would."

"But this doesn't prevent you from leaving your apartment. You sitting here is evidence of that. The reason you do not fear death on a daily basis is because the odds are quite low. But now your life has approached a crossroads of sorts — you may choose to stay in this city and face whatever consequences may come to you, or you can travel to Tri-City and face those consequences. Which do you think offers the highest probability of avoiding death?"

"Neither."

"Then it is up to you how you wish do die."

"Wait, that's it?" Kade responded. "That's your advice?"

"I have given you my advice, which if you recall was to make the trip. You can analyse all your fears and calculate the probabilities of each of those outcomes becoming a reality, factoring in unknown variables of course."

"I'm sorry, I'm not too quick on my feet. Can you please repeat what you said in simpler terms?"

"Traveling to Tri-City comes with risk, right?"

"Yes, I'm with you so far."

"Each of these risks is not guaranteed to happen, but come with a certain probability of happening."

"Okay."

"So, my advice to you is to choose the path in which you can control the most, and do whatever you can to mitigate the risks. Stack the odds so to speak so that the probability leads more in your favour."

"What do you mean? I mean, I understand what you're saying, but what do you suggest I do?"

"You mentioned weapons and transport are among your top concerns, did you not? I can help you with both."

"Help me how?"

"Faster bike, bigger weapons, accompaniment, whatever you need."

"You would do this for me?"

"As I'm sure your friend here has mentioned, I'm quite resourceful. If there is something you need, I can procure it for you."

"For a fee?"

"Of course, I'm not a charity," Mr. Chu chuckled.

"What kind of fee?"

"Depends on what you need from me."

"Okay, I appreciate that."

"So then it has been decided, with my help, you will travel to Tri-City."

"I guess so. I don't really feel like I have much of a choice, do I?"

"No, you don't," Mr. Chu laughed again. Kade wasn't in the mood for humour.

"So when can I see you again?" Kade asked.

"If I could give you one other piece of advice, I would suggest you get in contact with Mr. Saigon as soon as possible and let him know you've reconsidered his offer."

"I will. Thank you so much, Mr. Chu."

"It was my pleasure."

"In return, you will owe me a favour. When the time comes,
I will collect."

Chapter Seven

It was unusual for Kade to miss one of his NA meetings, which worried Tanjoban. He tried contacting Kade several times throughout the night, but there was no response. Fidgeting in his seat, he feared the worst.

Leaving the meeting early, Tanjoban went over to Kade's apartment and saw that the door had been forced open, breaking the air-tight seal and allowing precious oxygen to escape.

Not wanting to inadvertently step into the middle of a situation, Tanjoban proceeded with caution. He removed a small blade from his jacket and held it firmly in his hand. With his other hand, he slowly pushed the door open wide enough for him to slip through. He waited for a brief moment in the entryway to listen for any commotion that would signal the intruders were still in his apartment. When he didn't hear anything, he proceeded inside.

As he walked down the hall, he read the digital display in his helmet. There was only one body detected in the vicinity and the oxygen levels were dangerously low. Rounding the corner, he saw Kade lying on the floor with his face bloodied and bruised. He was unconscious and barely breathing.

"Kade!" Tanjoban said, rushing over to his wounded friend.

It was difficult to fully assess the damage since Kade's face was a bloody mess. Tanjoban looked around and saw that the apartment was completely trashed. He wasn't sure if this was a burglary, or payback from Mr. Saigon. Regardless, his friend needed help.

Reaching into his pocket, Tanjoban pulled out an Epipen and jabbed it into Kade's thigh. The injected liquid entered his bloodstream and took affect instantly. Kade's body spasmed as it desperately clung to life.

Kade's eyes slowly peeled open and he began to moan.

"You're okay, buddy?" Tanjoban said. "I got you."

Using the density scanner on his helmet, Tanjoban checked for any broken bones. Fortunately, there didn't appear to be any major fractures. For now, Kade was just in a lot of pain, but he would heal.

"Don't try to move," Tanjoban said. "Just relax. Can I get you anything?"

"In the kitchen. Third drawer down. By the fridge."

Before Kade could finish his sentence, Tanjoban was on his feet and dashing toward the kitchen.

"There's a bottle of pain killers. Bring me two please."

"Don't worry, I got you, buddy," Tanjoban said, filling up a glass of water and bringing the medicine to Kade. He knelt down beside his friend. With Tanjoban's help, Kade sat up and swallowed the pills.

"Can you breathe okay?" Tanjoban asked.

"It's a little stuffy in here, but I should be alright for a while."

"Where's your helmet? We should get you some oxygen. It'll help you heal and make you feel better."

"Over there," Kade pointed to a shelf. Sitting on the floor with his back against his couch, he took a deep breath. Within minutes, the oxygen and pain killers kicked in and he felt a lot better.

"What happened?" Tanjoban asked.

"I'll give you one guess?"

"You know what, I'm sick of Saigon, bro. I say we roll up on him and blast that fool."

"As much as I would love to live that dream with you, we can't... he has my mum."

"What!?"

"He said if I ever want to see her again, I have to do exactly what he says."

"I thought you called him and told him you reconsidered his offer?"

"I did. I guess I waited too long."

"So he gets your message, but still lays a beating on you?"

"Pretty much."

"That's messed up, bro."

"Yeah, well... no sense dwelling on it now."

"Man, I hate that guy. One of these days I swear he'll get what's coming to him."

"It gets worse," Kade said.

"You get beat within an inch of your life, your sweet mother gets kidnapped, and you're forced to do a suicide mission to Tri-City. How could it possibly get worse?"

"He got me high on ghost."

Tanjoban stood up and paced back and forth, fuming with rage.

"Yeah, his goon squad held me down and forced that toxin into my system."

"Why the hell would he do that?"

"No clue."

"He's pure evil. One year of sobriety down the drain. Does it still count if you get high against your will?"

"That's the least of my concerns right now. I have to deliver that package in one week. If I don't, my mother is dead."

"Can't you just kill Saigon and get your mother back?"

"It'd be easier to just deliver the package. I need to go talk to Chu, see if he can hook me up with some gear."

"Good thing you've been smart with your finances."

"Actually, I'll need a loan. Saigon and his men robbed me of my entire stash."

Tanjoban put his head down and exhaled. His friend's predicament kept getting worse, and there was nothing he could do about it. "I'm so sorry, brother. I can help you as much as I can, but as you know, I'm not as diligent with my savings as you are. Plus, I haven't been getting as many big jobs lately so I don't have much to offer."

"It's alright, buddy. I'll figure this out on my own."

"So when do you leave?"

"As soon as I can stand. The clock is ticking."

Chapter Eight

Kade was badly wounded and had no time to heal. Every moment that passed was one step closer to him and his mother suffering an unspeakable fate.

Coming down from his hit of ghost, he was already feeling immense cravings for his next fix. He had been clean for over a year now and was not sure how he wanted to handle that situation, especially while embarking on the most dangerous mission of his life. Going through withdrawal presented all sorts of problems.

Kade passed by three ghost heads on his way to Chu's Wisely, but didn't bother to stop. Walking with a slight limp, he entered the coffee shop and scanned in. Mr. Chu wasn't expecting Kade to return so soon, but was delighted to see him.

"Mr. Casey, welcome back," he said. "What can I get you, the usual?"

As with most shops, customer service agents were a relic of the past. While Mr. Chu's coffee shop was automated as well, he liked to spend his time there, interacting with guests.

"If the usual is a new bike and weapons, than yeah."

Mr. Chu looked around before discreetly nodding and inviting Kade into the back. Kade followed a few paces behind.

"You're limping," Chu commented. "You take a spill out there on your bike?"

"Not exactly."

"I take it your meeting with Saigon did not go well."

"No... no it did not."

Kade and Chu entered a small service elevator, which took them down to the basement. That's when Kade pulled off his helmet, revealing his bruised and swollen face. He had a busted lip and a cut over his right eye. Chu took notice.

"You should see the other guy," Kade said ironically.

Chu stared at him for a moment and then burst out laughing. "That was a good one. You're a very funny guy."

It was a lame joke as old as time, so Kade wasn't sure why Chu found it so funny.

"So you need a new motorcycle and some guns?"

"Yes, can you help me?"

"Of course, of course," Chu said smiling. "You've come to the right place. Mr. Chu can get you anything. But, there's one thing."

"Oh yeah, what's that?" Kade asked, expecting some outlandish condition.

"Last time we spoke, you said you were going to call Saigon and accept the job."

"Yeah."

"Why then did he hurt you?"

"I guess he didn't get the message. Not really important now, is it?"

"Did he take your bike too?"

"No, but my bike is old and may not make the trip. I need something with a lot more power. Something fast and can handle the harsh terrain. Something with gadgets. It's like you said, for a trip like this, I want to stack the odds in my favour."

"There are delivery trucks that routinely make this trip to Tri-City – they carry everything from passengers to supplies. Why doesn't Saigon just use one of those?"

"You know, I forgot to ask as he was stomping my head in. He's your old buddy, why don't you ask him?"

"Okay, okay, let's not dwell on matters that are outside of our control. You said you need weapons too?"

"Yes, do you have any?"

"Please, don't insult me. I have everything. What did you have in mind?"

"Something small, but packs a punch."

"Okay, so a powerful bike with gadgets and a small weapon that packs a punch. Got it. When do you need it by?"

"Yesterday."

Again, Mr. Chu laughed hysterically like it was the funniest thing he had ever heard.

"Okay, wait right here. I'll make a call."

Kade took a seat in the coffee shop while he waited for Mr. Chu to procure the items he requested. The coffee only served to enhance his desire for ghost. He fought the urge and focused on the cup in front of him. When he finished that, and the refill, he began to be overwhelmed with boredom. His feet were twitching and his arms began to tingle. Worst of all, he had a dull headache, which grew in intensity by the minute. Through deep breaths and other relaxation techniques, he tried to ignore the insatiable pull back to the dark side.

He buried his head in his arms, which were folded over each other on the table. His mind continued its decent as he slipped further into a state of despair and dependency. In such a weakened condition, he was not capable of making rational choices of his own volition. The drug had taken over and he was on the verge of becoming a full-blown ghost head junkie again.

Eventually, he could no longer fight the withdrawal symptoms and he submitted to temptation. His head snapped up like a man possessed and he shot out of his seat. Placing his helmet on his head, he cranked the oxygen on full blast. He closed his eyes, inhaled a deep breath, and then opened them again.

He marched outside with a confident swagger and headed East toward one of the ghost heads he had passed by earlier.

"Hey, pal," he said. "You selling?"

"Whatchu need?"

"Ghost," Kade said, looking over his shoulder. Drugs weren't illegal, but they instilled paranoia and delusions. An irrational fear was just one of many mind-altering states of the drug.

"How much you need?"

"Give me 100cc... no 200... actually make it 300."

"You sure?"

"Yeah."

"Okay, 300 it is. That'll be 600 units."

As soon as the transaction was done, Kade found himself in a private area behind the coffee shop. He sat on the dirty pavement, away from prying eyes, and he took out one capsule of ghost. He stared at the capsule and couldn't believe he was in this place once again.

Ghost was a drug that could be taken on its own or mixed with oxygen to give a person feelings of invincibility, recklessness, and euphoria. It was highly addictive and often used as a way of escape. It was developed after the fallout when people lost nearly everyone they ever cared about — not just family and friends, but their favourite restaurants, musicians, and entertainers. They lost their ability to cope and needed a substance to deal with the pain. There were no more celebrations or backyard BBQs, no more vacations or promotions, and early retirement took on a whole new meaning. Society went into a smokey, red-alert, mayday tailspin. In an instant, hopes and dreams were gone and life became a countdown until the end. There was nothing much to live for. People now focused on doing whatever they could to survive.

The mind of an addict was a terrible state to be in and Kade vowed to never touch the substance again. Yet, through circumstances beyond his control, the evil talons of the drug had sunk its claws in and had an inescapable influence on him. It took everything in his power to stand up and walk away, but that's what he decided to do.

Despite having just paid an arm and a leg for three capsules, he knew if he went down that path, he may never return.

Chapter Nine

Kade received a message from Mr. Chu informing him that his gear had arrived. He walked across the street and met Mr. Chu in front of his shop.

"That was fast," Kade said.

"What did I tell you? I can get you anything."

"The bike came in?" Kade asked as they made their way into the back.

"Wait till you see this thing."

"What did you get?"

"You'll see," Mr. Chu teased.

When they entered the back loading bay, Kade nearly lost his mind. In front of him was a mint Suicide 1200x — all black with thick treads. The bike was the fastest and most expensive bike ever produced.

"I can't believe it," Kade said, approaching the bike in awe. He studied every inch of it and ran his hands over all the surfaces. "I have only read about these things. How did you get this?"

"Mind you, this bike is no ordinary 1200x," Mr. Chu said with a satisfied smile. "No, this is no stock bike. It has every mod you can imagine. Suped-up motor with turbo boost, reinforced suspension, Kevlar-armoured panels, ultra-grip tires, carbon fibre frame, extra storage for your long-distance trip."

"Mr. Chu, this is incredible. Seriously, I can't believe you got me this."

Mr. Chu and Kade continued to circle the bike. Mr. Chu then put his thumb on a hidden sensor, which caused four panels to open, each had a small gun protrude. He pressed the sensor again and the guns retracted and the panels sealed up inconspicuously.

"Whoa! That was incredible," Kade said. The smile never left his face.

"There's a sensor right here," Mr. Chu explained. "Just put your thumb here. You can also open through a voice command in your helmet. But that's not even the best part. The guns are automated so all you have to do is drive and they do the rest. You set the target and they will lock on."

"That's so cool."

"Wait, there's more," Mr. Chu said, leading Kade to the rear of the bike. "See this compartment? Inside is a Midnight Raven Drone — top of the line. Deploy it at will and see the visuals pop-up in the display of your helmet."

"Does it have guns on it too?"

"No, but it can carry heavy loads, which may come in handy."

"Good to know. This thing is amazing, Mr. Chu."

"There's one other thing. This bike can drive itself. It has sensors that make thousands of decisions per second, far better than a human driver. No offense."

"None taken."

"To activate it, just press this button and then you can use your voice to command it."

"Incredible," Kade said, truly astonished. It made his bike seem like it belonged in a museum.

"Now, let me show you the guns I got for you."

Kade was overwhelmed and quite excited to test out his new gear. After Mr. Chu showed him the guns and how to use everything, they had an important discussion about price. Kade was almost afraid to ask. However, seeing the bike and all its capabilities, he knew he couldn't make the trip without it.

"So, Mr. Chu, for the bike, the weapons, and all the other gear, what are we talking?"

"For now, they are my gift to you," Mr. Chu said.

"What do you mean, 'for now'? I don't want to have some impossible debt to pay when I come back."

"You don't have to take the deal, it's up to you."

Kade was trapped and knew that without the bike and weapons, he was dead man. Whatever debt he had to settle in the future was best not to think about at this time. Mr. Chu had a reputation of being fair and straightforward, so he bowed to him and told him he would accept the deal.

"Good luck, Kade."

"Thank you, Mr. Chu... for everything."

Chapter Ten

Kade hit the open road. His new bike felt much lighter and faster than the one he previously had. With his oxygen cranked, he cruised through the night, relying on the sensors on his bike to navigate through the thick smog. Since people rarely travelled, not even by air, the highways were mostly empty, which was a bonus. The first two hours of the journey were not the dangerous part. The danger would come later.

His fatigued brain kept replaying the images of the attack from the night before. Now less than twenty-four hours later, it felt surreal that he was on the first leg of the trip that he feared so much.

***

It happened a little after midnight, Kade was awoken by a loud crash and the sound of men charging into his apartment. The door of his apartment had been kicked in, breaking the air seal. Kade jumped up and went for his gun, but was met with a boot to the chest. He flew back on the couch and before he could get up, three men were pummeling him.

As the air escaped his apartment and replaced with poisonous carbon dioxide, Kade began to gasp for breath. He scrambled toward his helmet, but was held in place by three angry men.

One of the men scanned every wall in his apartment until he found what he was looking for. On one of the walls were the greasy smears of hand prints, indicating there was a hidden panel that was operated by a touch sensor.

As his mind wandered, images continued to flash in his head.

One of the thug's broken into the secret stash and removed all his preciously preserved canisters. He returned to the living room where his cohorts were handily strong-arming Kade into submission. Any reservations from backing out of the deal were completely gone.

"I can't... brea—" Kade struggled with his words through a busted up jaw.

"Let him go," Saigon said, entering the apartment. "He's no use to us dead."

The man let Kade go and then kicked over Digi.

"I called you," Kade said, barely able to breathe.

"You did?" Mr. Saigon said. He then took his phone out and played the message.

"Playing message form Kade Casey — 'Mr. Saigon, I hope this message finds you well. I have reconsidered your offer and decided to take you up on it. I can leave as soon as possible.' — end of message. To replay message, press 1."

"Oh, I guess you did. So I guess all this was unnecessary then. Oops, my bad. In any event, it appears we're on the same page now. Oh and Mr. Casey... we'll hold on to your mother just in case you decide to change your mind. Deliver the package and you can see your mum again. Sound good?"

Kade did his best to block out those thoughts, but on these solo adventures, the mind tended to wander into the darkest corners.

***

"Mum, look at me!" Kade said, standing on the seat of his bike.

Kade's mother watched her son proudly standing in her perfectly manicured lawn surrounded by a white picket fence. Kade was in the street, on his bike, showing off all the tricks he could do. The sky was blue, the weather was warm, and a slight breeze kept them cool.

"Very nice, Kaden."

"When's dad coming home?"

"He won't be home until later. He's working a night shift again. You can see him tomorrow afternoon."

"Ah-man," Kade complained, taking a wide turn around the cul-de-sac before coming to a stop. "Okay, mum, watch this one. I'm going to jump off that curb and spin my handlebars."

"Okay, I'm watching."

Kade beamed with joy because he could show off to his captive audience of one. He placed all his weight on his front, setting the bike in motion. He furiously peddled toward the curb with a fierce look of intensity. His bike rocked back and forth as he rode high like a jockey. His front wheel hit the lip of the curb, he popped off, and became momentarily airborne. Maintaining his focus, he whipped the handlebars around so that it, along with the front wheel, rotated 360 degrees before catching it again and sticking the landing.

The bike came down with a thunderous crash and as the wheels touched down, the entire ground shook. With a look of shock, Kade settled the bike and came to a stop. When he looked back at his mother to see if she had witnessed his trick, she was looking up at the sky in horror. Kade turned his head around and saw a large plume of smoke engulf the sky.

The ground started to shake and Kade's mum quickly called him over to come back inside their pristine suburban home.

****

Kade snapped out of his daze and focused on the hazards ahead. On either side of him were hundreds of kilometres of scorched Earth. Since the eruption of Eldorado super volcano nearly two decades ago, the world, along with civilization was forever changed. The once luscious planet, with green trees and blue skies, was in a desperate state of decay where nothing grew, and nature resembled a mars-like surface.

The initial blast wiped out everything in a hundred-kilometre radius, but what happened next did even more damage. The sky turned black, restricting the sunlight. This sent the world into a cataclysmic shift, which killed nearly every living thing on the planet.

The remaining survivors quickly scrambled, gathering food, supplies, and finding safe refuge. Some had prepped for a disaster such as this and retreated into their underground bunkers, while others seal their windows and doors, and relied on air filters to keep them alive.

With time, the dust began to settle and people started venturing out into the world. Essential services such as grocery stores and hospitals resumed operation. People left their houses only when necessary, ensuring they covered their mouths with anything from coffee filters to diapers just to filter the particles out of the air.

Adjusting to a new normal, the resilience of humans found a way to carry on. New manufacturing plants and services emerged. High-tech masks and helmets became as ubiquitous as smartphones. People now breathed out of oxygen canisters and had home filtration systems installed. Along with these changes in lifestyle, people also saw old systems and governments collapse, giving rise to new power dynamics. Mr. Saigon had become the richest and most powerful man in the city.

Chapter Eleven

What made the route to Tri-City so dangerous was that there was no route. Traversing the badlands, as they were called, was more like completing a video game. First level was the dunes, then the ruins, the sinkholes, the mountains, the desert, the then the pit. Each level posed their own sets of challenges.

The dunes were the first checkpoint that was notorious for wreaking havoc on vehicles. The soft sand would clog up moving parts and cause tires to get stuck.

The ruins had miles of hazardous debris and scavengers — a lawless group of bandits that would stop at nothing to get their hands on anything of value. They were mostly after oxygen — the pure stuff. They were clever too, setting traps and relentlessly pursuing their targets, forcing them to panic and make mistakes. More often than not, people travelling through these parts never made it passed the ruins.

For those luckily enough to survive the first two parts were met with a long stretch covered in sinkholes — large openings in the Earth loosely concealed with sand and rock. Even a small sinkhole could kill a traveller if they were unfortunate enough to fall in. The larger holes were easier to avoid, but the surrounding area was just as unstable. Even the slightest weight or disturbance could cause the ground to shift and collapse without warning. If the fall wasn't enough to kill a person, the subsequent rubble would bury them alive.

Next, was a steep ascent into the mountains. The treacherous climb through acid rain and snow weren't the only hazards. The sudden changes in weather, falling rock, broken roads, unstable bridges, and other passengers were just some of the things to watch out for.

Once through the mountains, travellers would be met with miles upon miles of desert. These parts weren't known to have any people, but the threats were endless. The hot climate, the freezing temperate drop at night, the sandstorms... any one could be enough to pose serious health risks or cause equipment failure.

Making it through these stages were actually the easiest part of the journey. As for the pit, Kade didn't want to even think about it until the time came.

There were no rest stops along the way, no hotels or restaurants, no mechanics that could help repair or replace broken parts, no creeks or lakes to drink from or wash up. A traveller was pretty much on their own — human vs. nature.

Unfortunately, there was only one way across.

At night, the temperature dropped to sub 30 degrees Celsius, but Kade's suit kept his body temperature stable — an upgrade from Mr. Chu. The suit also worked in hot climates as well, to keep his body cool. Without it, he would succumb to the elements.

Kade had been riding throughout the night, breathing a supply of pure oxygen, which aided his wakeful state. At a certain point he would have to stop and get proper rest. His body was used to being hunched over for long periods of time, but with the beating and the mental anguish he had endured, he was about ready to collapse.

He entered the dunes just as the sun was rising, which created the most picturesque beauty he had seen in a while. Seeing the gradient orange sky as the sun rose over the rolling mounds of sand was almost worth the trip. As the sun continued to rise, it would make the desert unbearable. Fortunately, Kade had all the proper gear he needed.

The road had run out over a kilometre ago, and Kade saw nothing but endless dunes in every direction. With a simple voice command, he launched his drone, which exploded out of the back of his bike and climbed to over two-hundred feet within seconds. Through his digital display, he got a topographical view of the landscape. As he had suspected, there were no places to rest or hide. There were no caves or trees casting shade, just a barren wasteland.

He reduced his speed and eventually came to a stop. After a quick systems check, he dismounted his bike and stretched his legs and back. The hydration system in his helmet was enough to last the trip, but only when he was connected to his bike. He had been slowly sipping it all night and had gotten used to it. Now he was ten paces away from his bike and had a slight moment of panic when he attempted to take a drink and nothing came out.

After relieving himself, he walked back to his bike, rehydrated, and then laid down for a quick nap. He had instructed his drone to continue to survey the area and alert him of any danger. Nestling into a grove in the sand, Kade closed his eyes and fell asleep almost instantly. He only needed a few hours sleep.

Near the end of his sleep cycle, Kade was awoken by a soft beeping sound. In a state of delirium, he forgot where he was and instinctually reached for his weapon. He posted up in a sitting position and looked ahead, but didn't see any danger. He checked the temperature and it was much lower than he was expecting. As he continued to become more awake and gather his senses, he noticed it was also much dimmer. Nevertheless, the alarm from the drone persisted.

He rose to his feet and looked behind him. He stood in awe for a moment at the sheer magnitude of what was coming toward him. A giant wall of sand that stretched skyward, blocking out the sun. It was a nasty storm with thunder and lighting, unlike anything he had ever experienced before. It caught him off guard.

He retrieved his drone and plotted out what he would do next. As he saw it, there were only three options — outrun it, stay put and hunker down, or ride into it. It made little sense to head back in the direction in which he had come. There was also no way around it. In that moment, he heard a voice in his head. It was Mr. Chu telling him to analyse the situation and stack the odds in his favour. There was no need to take unnecessary risks and riding blindly into a giant sand storm on a bike just didn't seem like a wise decision.

If he was going to ride out the storm, he needed to act quickly. He mounted his bike and rode to the largest dune he could find and parked on the opposite side as the storm. He then took out a cable from a compartment on his bike and buried one end into the ground as deep as possible. On the end of the cable were spikes that stuck out like a grapple and acted as a land anchor. The cable was intended to be a winch, but he had to improvise. As the storm grew nearer, he tipped his bike on top of him, creating some sort of barrier of protection, and then got into a fetal position.

The thunderous winds swept over the dune, creating a noise so loud that he could hardly hear himself think. Now fully engulfed in the swirling debris of chaos. He felt the bike move and expected it to be ripped from the ground and tossed around like a plastic bag. However, taking refuge behind one of the dunes seemed to have sheltered him from the strong gusts of wind. Now all he had to worry about was being buried alive.

The storm seemed never-ending. He laid in one spot, covered in sand, for over an hour. His helmet was completely covered, blocking out his vision, but fortunately he could still breathe. Through his heads-up display, he was able to monitor everything from the wind and temperature. Once the winds slowed down and the temperature began to climb, he knew the storm had passed and the sun was now out.

A heavy blanket of sand covered him, restricting his movements. He struggled, pushed and kicked, but with each movement, it seemed to only make him more stuck. Claustrophobia was an issue for him, and for a brief moment he felt like he could die there. Less than 24 hours into his trip, the harsh environment had nearly taken him out. He needed to think of a solution, quickly.

He felt around and found the cable. He then remembered Mr. Chu telling him the bike could go on autopilot from voice commands. He spoke the command, "Bike, drive ten feet."

The bike came to life and the thick tires found traction in the soft sand. Instantly, he could feel the ground move around him. Still holding onto the cable, the bike centered itself and pulled him out the dune, dragging him across the sand for ten feet before coming to a stop.

"That was cool."

Chapter Twelve

With his drone flying high above him, he continued on course making considerable progress. He had survived the dunes and the nasty sand storm. The next stage of his journey was the abandoned city.

After riding several hours in the golden sands, he was beginning to be lulled into a false sense of security. So far there were relatively few dangers on his voyage. He had an insanely fast bike with every gadget imaginable, was one of the most skilled riders in the world, and was heavily armed. The more he thought about the dangers, the more confident he became.

In his heads-up display, Kade was alerted to movement several kilometers ahead. As he approached closer, he was able to get more information. When he was less than a hundred yards away, he was able to pick up the digital signature of a woman. A silhouette of a slender woman appeared along with some basic biometric data — approximate height, weight, and BMI. This was far less information than what most digital signatures looked like, especially with Kade's equipment. He was usually able to bypass the privacy settings and see nearly every detail about a person. However, her signature was wiped clean, which was a red flag.

Kade wondered what she was doing all the way out in the middle of the desert by herself, without any transportation or supplies, barely able to stand. Kade was clever to these sorts of tactics — some cute damsel pretends to be in distress, waiting for some poor sap to come along and rescue her. She was surely bait for a trap that Kade had no intention of falling for.

As he passed her, she began frantically waving before collapsing face first. Kade raced passed her in a flash until she became just another blip on his radar. A slight smirk came across his face as he uttered to himself, "Nice try."

Kade continued on, but then thought about what his mother would do. His moral compass kept drawing him to the woman. 'What if she truly needed help?' he thought. 'Nah.' Kade then thought about his mother and the woman on the street. He continued to go back and forth in his mind until his conscience got the better of his rationality.

He slowed to a stop and looked around. He was on the outskirts of the dunes and could see the abandoned city ahead. 'Where did this woman come from?' he thought. 'Who or what is she running from?' Kade checked the time.

A large holographic timer appeared in his display, giving the illusion that it was projected ten feet in front of him. Each second that passed reminded him that he didn't have a lot of time to spare.

'If she were part of a trap, then where are the others?' he wondered. There weren't any others around and she did not appear to be armed. He kept debating.

Kade readjusted on his bike, spun it around in the sand, creating a large rooster tail, and took off in the direction he had just come from. Against his better judgement, he just couldn't live with himself if she truly was in need of his help. 'If I'm a sap, then I'm a heavily armed sap.'

As he approached the woman, he reduced his speed. She was lying face down and not moving. He parked his bike, dismounted, and withdrew his weapon. Looking around, he approached with caution. There really weren't any places to hide, which set his mind at ease. If she came from where he was going, then perhaps she could provide him with valuable information.

'Are you okay?' he spoke into his helmet. The audio file along with a chat request was sent instantly to the girl. He could tell she accepted the message and listened to it. A connection was established as he hung back about twenty feet, on high alert for any surprises that may come up. He didn't have to wait long until a reply came back. He accepted the message and a soft voice permeated throughout his helmet. 'Please, I need help. Water.'

Kade analyzed those five words before responding, looking for any clue that she may be being deceitful.

"What are you doing out here?" he asked.

"I was a prisoner, held captive, but I escaped."

"What kind of prisoner? Who held you captive?"

"I'll tell you whatever you want to know," the woman moaned in desperation. "Please, I need water."

Kade sat with those words and he was in a moral conundrum. Any sort of slip up or misjudgment on this journey could not only cost him his life, but also his mother's. He already knew he was going to help her or else he wouldn't have come back. He couldn't just turn around and leave her to die. There weren't a lot of travellers in these parts and if she truly needed water, she would likely die before another traveller came by.

"I can give you water, but only a little," he said.

"Thank you."

"In exchange, I need you to tell me everything you know about the road up ahead."

"Yes, of course. I can tell you whatever you want to know — who's out there, the traps, the best route, the best places to hide."

Water came in little packs that were stored in his bike, he couldn't exactly just give her a drink from a water bottle. Besides, in this environment, everyone wears helmets and would never expose their face to take a drink of water.

"Okay look," Kade said. "I have water in my bike. I'm also packing a Wind Blazer. If you try anything, I won't hesitate to blast you across this desert.

"It's okay, you can trust me. My word is gold."

Kade returned to his bike and drove toward the young lady, parking mere inches from where she was lying. Kade once again dismounted and helped the young woman to her feet.

"You're my hero," she said. "I cannot thank you enough."

The woman mounted Kade's bike and connected the drinking tube to her helmet. "I'm not sure how much good this will do," he said. "It's sort of delaying the inevitable. You won't survive long without water."

"Hopefully, I will meet another nice traveller such as yourself. If I keep doing that, I can make it the whole way like that."

"How's your oxygen?" he asked.

"I have enough for two days."

"That's not enough. Let me top you up."

"You have a good heart."

"You can thank my mother," he said, letting his guard down and feeling a little more at ease about the situation. "My name's Kade, what's your name?"

Before the woman answered, she shoved a taser into his thigh and zapped him. The high-intensity voltage pulsated throughout his body and he lost all control of his muscles. He toppled over like a bag of sand, dropping his gun in the process, and continued convulsing in the sand. Despite all his precaution, he had been tricked.

The pain was unbearable and left his body in a momentary state of paralysis. His thoughts scrambled almost as if his soul had become separated from his body.

As the feeling slowly started to return, he writhed on the ground in pain and completely helpless. His muscles eventually regained some functionality and he turned onto his stomach and pushed himself up to his knees. He staggered to his feet like a new born giraffe, swaying back and forth until the feeling in his muscles returned. Through heavy blinks and a pulsating headache, he had the wherewithal to reach for his weapon. It was gone. With the steadiness of a ventriloquist dummy, he stood with a feeling of stupidity as he watched the women disappear from his sight.

As the female rider raced off with his bike, Kade was more than a little annoyed. She was killing precious time. Having a stretch and cracking his neck, he began to decompress. He then tracked various displays in his visor as his eyes darted back and forth, looking at data as it populated. After a few seconds, a black dot appeared in the distance.

Kade stood relaxed, with his arms by his side and exhaling a deep breathe. The woman raced toward him at blurring speed, enhanced by the hazy heat waves of a desert mirage. The bike was almost completely soundless. The black dot grew larger as it approached closer, appearing as if it was on course to plow into him, but Kade didn't flinch. The female rider on the other hand was completely unaware of the bike's abilities to be guided remotely. The bike slowed to a stop directly in front of Kade. In a calm voice and demeanour, he commanded, "Get off. Now."

There was no need to check to see if the precious cargo was still in place, it was located in a small concealed compartment, air-sealed and locked.

"Oh come on, I was just taking it for test drive, I didn't know you would be so sensitive about it."

Kade held his hand out and demanded the gun. Without hesitation, the woman returned it to him. She could have refused, but in that moment, she decided to cooperate.

She dismounted the bike in a huff and stepped aside.

"Back up," Kade commanded, now aiming his weapon at her head.

"What are you doing?" she desperately pleaded. "You can't just leave me out here. Come on, man."

Without saying another word to her, Kade mounted his bike and took off toward the abandoned city, leaving her in a cloud of dust.

"Kade!" she yelled. It was no use, he was gone.

Kade cut the communication link and never thought about her again. It served him right for getting involved in someone else's business. He vowed to never make that mistake again. With a determined look in his eye, Kade narrowed his brow and focused on the abandoned city, which was fast approaching. Unfortunately, he didn't get any intel from the woman that could help him navigate the streets and avoid threats.

Unlike the Hive city in which he had passed through a thousand times, he had no idea what hazards may lie ahead. It presented a whole different set of obstacles than the dunes. It was less about environmental hazards and more about people with bad intentions. He recalled the little information the desert woman relayed to him, which was that there were bad people, optimal and sub-optimal routes, and places to hide. After all, she supposedly came from these ruins, so there were obviously people living there. That information alone was enough to cause concern.

Chapter Thirteen

Kade brought his bike to a stop just on the outskirts of the city limits. Receiving information from his drone, he scouted the best route. The city was too large to go around. It would also be too time consuming. Heading straight through the city was the shortest and most obvious path; however, also likely to be the most dangerous.

With no time to spare, Kade set off. Even though his bike hardly made a sound, that was of little consequence. Whoever were in these empty streets had other ways of detecting travellers passing through.

Entering the abandoned city was yet another sobering thought of humanity's fragility. Countless blocks of blown out high-rises and decaying structures, empty parks and lifeless suburbs, all covered in a thick layer of ash. The city was a ghost town, a lost and forgotten skeleton of what was a once vibrant and prosperous hub for civilization.

Kade's drone stayed ahead of him, scanning the streets. So far, the coast was clear. His eyes scanned the streets and buildings as well. There were far too many places to hide, which made him feel exposed and vulnerable. He stuck to side streets and travelled at a moderate speed just so that if a hazard were to present itself suddenly and unexpectedly, he would have enough time to react.

Following his drone, Kade pulled into a parkade located under a random office building. He crept in, driving passed a number of broken down and rusted vehicles that were half buried in dust and debris. There didn't appear to be any other tracks in the dirt, which was a good sign. He pulled around a corner, placing sensors as he went, until he found a hidden spot tucked away in the back that made him feel safe. According to the drone's digital scan, there were multiple entry and exit points so in case of an attack, he could make an escape.

Kade dismounted after a long day of riding and laid down on the dirt-covered floor. It was another chance to catch a few much needed hours of rest. He was on a tight schedule and had only allotted a few hours of sleep per day.

He checked the timer, which had been counting down from five days. He also had a map, which charted his course so that he could visually see how far he was to his final destination. After being on the road for less than twenty-four hours, he still had a long way to go.

He had a quick meal, holding his breath and lifting up his
helmet just enough so that he could take a bite of a high-
caloric protein bar. He then lowered his helmet back down
to chew. He did this several times until it was finished. It
wasn't exactly the best source of nutrients, but it was the
customary food source for riders on the go.

Another hunger that persisted was his insatiable desire to
take a hit of ghost. He still had a small vile of it and kept the
thought in his mind at all times. He wrestled with the idea of
throwing it away, and on several occasions reached the
conclusion that it was best to discard it, but something
always prevented him from doing it. The drug had an
incredible pull on him that was hard to shake. His rationale
was it was better to have it and not need it than it was to
need it and not have it.

Kade settled in, exhaling and relaxing his mind and body.
Within a few minutes, he was asleep.

Less than an hour into his rest, his alarm blared in his ears,
alerting him of danger. In his sleep-depraved state, he had
momentarily forgotten where he was. He looked around the
underground parking structure and began to gain his
bearings. A soft light crept in from a large crack in one of the
walls, providing enough light for him to see. There were no
signs of danger. He looked in his visor, but didn't see
anything.

He quickly mounted his bike and began to pull away, but was blindsided by an electrical pulse that knocked him off his bike and sent him flying into a parked car. The door caved in on impact and he was once again lying on the soot covered floor. Unsure what had hit him, he attempted to crawl to safety, but the pain was crippling.

The small clan of nomadic scavengers had tracked him down and had him surrounded. The scavies, as they were called, were a lawless group usually with primitive technology. But these people were from a different tribe and could not be compared to any others. They had stolen high-tech weapons from travellers and were looking to do the same with him.

Another shot exploded near his head, sending debris on top of him and chills down his spine. It was too close for comfort.

The shots kept coming in multiple directions and Kade had yet to fully regain his faculties. The noise was deafening. Loud flashes of light exploded all around him. A nearby car was blasted to bits and sharp chunks of metal rained down on him.

Kade withdrew his weapon, but was barely able to raise his arm let alone steady it to take aim. The gun had a kick, which required a certain level of strength to withstand the resistance. The only thing that didn't hurt was to speak. Using a voice command, he launched his drone from the back of his bike. It raced around the perimeter obtaining a digital scan of the area. Now, Kade had a rudimentary visual map showing him the location and number of his attackers.

He slid back down and continued to watch the blips on his display as they circled in closer. With time, Kade slowly regained movement in his limbs and crawled to safety behind a heap of rubble. With his back now against a wall, he attempted to use it to push himself up to his feet. A paralyzing jolt of residual electricity flashed through his fried nervous system and caused him to grit his teeth in agony.

There was one more option that Kade had in mind, but he only wanted to use it as a last resort. Reaching into his jacket, he pulled out a hit of ghost and stared at it. Now was not the time for hesitation. His life was on the line and he needed to make a quick decision.

Chapter Fourteen

Kade was about to cross a line he hoped he wouldn't have to cross. Holding a small dose of the drug, he connected the tiny canister of ghost to his helmet and let the liquid turn to vapour. He closed his eyes and inhaled deeply. The drug mixed with the oxygen and entered his bloodstream via his lungs. After a few deep breaths, he disconnected the empty canister and waited for the drug to take effect.

He could feel it work almost instantly. His body went numb and he stood up with confidence. With his blaster in his hand, he fought back like outlaw. He let out three shots from his supersonic weapon and hit all three targets. Dust and debris filled his field of vision and created a visual barrier.

He walked over to his bike, picked it up of the ground, and hopped on. Within seconds of taking the drug, his demeanour had changed. The euphoric feeling of invincibility was exactly what he needed in this scenario and reminded him why he became so addicted to it in the first place.

Kade took off in the direction in which he had come, navigating through the underground facility and avoiding any threats. Ducking his head and swerving around fallen objects, he sped away. The entire underground facility filled with a thick cloud of ash that had been disturbed. With a simple voice command, hidden panels on the front of his bike opened up to reveal two guns. The guns had sensors that looked for targets. When the targets were locked, Kade made the final decision to discharge the blasts. Several rounds of high-frequency sonic blasters pulsated out of the guns in a precise manner, finding their targets and taking out several scavies with non-lethal force.

Sinking down in his riding mount, Kade create a low centre of gravity, which would help him control the bike as well as make himself a smaller target. The scavies shot back and but missed. With the exit in site, Kade and his drone shot out of the parkade like a canon and took to the streets. He became momentarily airborne, and when he landed, he shifted his weight and was heavy on the throttle. The backend fished-tailed out in the loose soot-covered streets before finding traction.

Fearing his drone would be shot down, Kade instructed it to dock. It was a risk because now he was driving blindly. The sensors on the bike picked up movement and blasted automatically as Kade kept his eyes on the road.

The bike raced through the desolate streets leaving the scavies in his dust. The effects of the ghost were now fully pulsating through his bloodstream, and he was in the zone. It allowed him to dial in and make thousands of micro decisions per second. With an expressionless face, he was in a sort of trance-like state where he had no fear.

Pulling the bike into a wheelie, Kade's reckless nature took over. As his front wheel regained contact with the ground, he swiveled his head around and saw a squad of scavies flooding out of the buildings like rats. Their torn, loose-fitted clothes draped off them like dirty rags, covering their entire bodies. Goggles covered their eyes and they wore crude breathing masks, which looked like they were pieced together from scraps.

The scavies screamed in unison like warriors on a hunt, but Kade was too focused to let it faze him. Besides, seeing as the scavies were on foot and he was on a bike, he wasn't at all concerned about them catching him.

Several scavies appeared from seemingly out of nowhere and from all angles. This time they were on motorbikes and other off-roading vehicles, which appeared to be assembled in a junkyard, sharing some semblance to a scene out of Mad Max.

Kade was a far more skilled rider and was on the best bike money could buy, so he was confident he could outrun and out-manoeuver them. The only advantage they had was that they knew the streets well and had even designed it with traps.

Kade began making a series of sporadic turns in an effort to be evasive. Left and right, Kade jockeyed back and forth as his silent bike moved stealthily through the streets, sliding around corners. So far, he was doing well to avoid capture.

At one point, he made a wrong turn and was met with a roadblock. This was the first inclination that the scavies may be leading him into a trap. Like a spider catching a flying, the more the prey would struggle, the more it would seal its fate.

'Maximize your odds,' he heard Chu's voice once again. If he were to outsmart the scavies, he needed to think two steps ahead and be unpredictable. Running was the obvious choice. Fighting seemed like a death wish. That only other option was to hide.

He came to a full stop and quickly turned around to look for another street. His eyes darted around, looking for a building in which he could enter. Less than fifty feet away, he found what he was looking for and accelerated toward a building. He entered through a hollowed-out window of what was once the main lobby. He manoeuvred around some debris and made his way up a flight of stairs. Soot and ash filled the stairs making it more like a ramp. The thick-treaded tires climbed the stairs with ease. Within seconds, he was on the second floor.

Flying down one of the hallways, Kade entered a random room. The large space was filled with old desks and cubicles, covered in soot. It was most likely an office for some company back in its heyday. Now, like everything, it resembled the aftermath of Chernobyl.

Looking at his timer, the seconds and minutes counted down. He didn't have time for this, but had no other options. Within the hour, his hit of ghost would slowly begin to wane, and he would experience intense symptoms of withdrawal, which he wasn't looking forward to. But it was an unavoidable byproduct of the drug. The only way to curb those effects were to take more. But he had no regrets. Had he not taken it, he may have been captured, or worse, killed.

Kade found shelter under a forgotten piece of furniture and closed his eyes. His hope was that in a few hours, the scavies would give up looking for him and he could continue to carry out his mission. There was nothing to do now, but to sit tight and wait it out.

Chapter Fifteen

With the exits blocked, the scavies knew their prey was hiding somewhere and they were hellbent on finding him. If they had to scour every building and every room to flush Kade out, they would. Time was on their side. They knew hiding was futile and he would have to come out eventually. Travellers always had a limited food, water, and oxygen.

Kade tried to catch some rest, but the drug was causing debilitating paranoia. He could hear loud bangs and the savage howls from the scavies in the streets below. They were relentless. He had underestimated their resolve and now that nightfall had set in, he had realized the crucial mistake he had made.

As the drug wore off, his mind played tricks on him. He would hallucinate, hear voices that were not there, and twitch for no reason. He was bugging out and desperately wanted to take another dose to keep the demons at bay. Plus, the pain from earlier was flaring up. His body had endured a beating and needed rest, but that was a luxury he could not afford.

Kade rose to his feet. In his sleep depraved, drug-induced brain, he wasn't able to think clearly. He commanded his drone to deploy from his bike and exit through one of the hundred smashed out windows. It would surveil on the grounds below and provide him valuable intel.

The drone zipped through the old office and flew above the skyline. As it cruised through the city, it picked up several figures, informing Kade exactly which areas to avoid and what was the best route to escape.

Glancing at the timer, he was approaching the twenty-four hour mark. He had six more days to go. Mounting his bike, he engaged his night vision. The entire building, and city for that matter, was pitch black. Nobody had seen the moon in years. Even on the clearest of nights, only a faint hazy circle was visible.

Kade silently rode his bike through a large set of doors and down the hall. The walls and other objects in his field of view lit up with green highlights, allowing him to navigate. He passed a set of inoperable elevators, making his way toward the stairs from which he came. He took a moment to double check the route and ensure it was still viable. Once the coast was clear, he descended the stairs and took off into the night.

Racing through the city, Kade followed the map in his display. The scavies appeared to be completely unaware of him, which brought a smirk to his face. He leaned into a turn as he rounded the block at high speed, nearly hugging the pavement. Before he could straighten out, he was yanked off his bike abruptly and unexpectedly, and brought to the ground with a thud. The wind had been knocked out of him and he desperately gasped for breathe.

His bike continued to ghost ride for several yards before crashing into the side of a building. Kade heard the loud crash, but was too hurt to pay any attention to it. He was in survival mode, writhing on the ground in more pain than he had ever felt. He wondered what the hell he had run into because he didn't see anything.

As he laid in the foreign streets, gasping for breath, a thick cable hovered above him. The cable that stretched across the street was painted black so that it was nearly undetectable at night.

Moaning on the ground, he slowly regained control of his breathing. He had his body armour to thank for keeping his bones from breaking. He cranked his oxygen to one hundred percent, which helped ease some of the pain.

Kade felt as though he was dying and there was no point to carry on. He had failed. There was nothing better to do than to allow the ghost to take him away and die with peace and dignity.

The scavies were like a pack of savage hyenas that would surely strip him naked and take anything of value without batting an eye and leave him in the streets to die. Since his bike was likely trashed and he could barely move, he knew he was likely lying in his final place of rest.

The celebratory howls of the scavies echoed throughout the streets as they circled around their prey.

Without hesitation, Kade injected his second hit of ghost and let it mix with the oxygen. The drug entered his lungs and gave him a second wind. He was hoping to space out the doses, but with three hits in the last twenty-four hours, he was now a full-blown junkie again. If he were to survive, this would definitely complicate matters for him.

Chapter Sixteen

When Kade regained consciousness, he was surprised to find himself alive — naked, but alive. Everything he owned had been stripped off of him.

Unsure where he was, he looked around, but could hardly see a thing. Within a minute, his eyes adjusted to the darkness. A small amount of light escaped the hallway outside his room and crept through the tiny sliver of space underneath the door to his cell. His body was sore all over and shivered from the cold that penetrated his body like a disease. To make matters worse, he also had a splitting headache, a result of the synthetic oxygen he had been breathing combined with the nasty spill he had taken. Trace amounts of ghost still flirted with his mind, creating a strange mental state in which he desperately wanted to escape.

Trapped in an eight by ten-foot cell with nothing but an empty bucket, he thought about his mother and hoped she was okay. His thoughts then drifted toward wondering why the scavies kept him alive, and how much time had passed. If he ever wanted to see his mother alive, he needed to find a way to break free from his cell, find his gear, and... before he could finish the thought, a wave of despair consumed him. Given his current status, that seemed like such an impossible feat.

Trying to keep from shaking, he curled up in the corner. After a couple of agonizing hours in solitude, he heard footsteps coming toward his door. Kade had his head buried in his folded arms and when the door opened, he looked up. A blast of light flooded the room and caused his eyes to squint. Standing in the doorway was the silhouette of a large figure – broad shoulders and a wide stance. Behind him were two other men dressed in typical scavie garb.

Kade's eyes adjusted to the light and he got a better look at the man. The man dressed much differently than the other scavies. With his modern helmet and battle armour, he looked more like a solider from the future.

"What's your name?" the man asked in a commanding voice.

"Kade... Kade Casey."

"Where are you from?"

"Megalopolis," he answered. "Endocrine district."

"Endocrine? Never heard of it," the man said. "What brings you to these parts?"

"I'm just passing through."

"You're a rider?"

"Yes."

"Riders make deliveries."

"Sometimes."

"Tell me Kade Casey from Endocrine... what were you delivering?"

"Like I said, I was just passing through. I decided to take some time off and do some exploring," Kade said with shallow breaths, shivering from the cold.

"Some exploring?"

"I figured I would make my way to Tri-city. Thinking about relocating."

"Get him up," the man commanded.

Two scavies funneled into the room and grabbed Kade under his armpits. They hauled him to his feet and brought him to the leader. Kade looked up at the man who was towering over him.

"I'll ask you again," the man spoke in a matter of fact way. He was used to using intimidation tactics to get people to do what he wanted. "What were you delivering?"

"It was a small package. I don't know what it was. I never ask. I had it in my bike... but it was stolen from me in the dunes. My contractor is a very powerful man. If he finds out I didn't deliver his package, he will kill me and people I care about. So I decided to continue on toward Tri-city with the intent on starting a new life. This is the truth. You can search my gear, I don't have any package."

The story was not entirely true, but seemed to satisfy the leader. The scavies checked the bike thoroughly and were unable to find any package. Before Kade was captured, he removed the package and had his drone hide it on a random rooftop. His hopes were that if he were to escape, he could recall the drone along with the package and carry on his way.

"This contractor you speak of... what's his name?"

"He goes by the name of Saigon," Kade said.

"Mr. Saigon," the man repeated, demonstrating familiarity with the name. "Interesting."

The man turned around and the scavies followed suit, unhanding Kade.

"Wait, where are you going?" Kade asked. "You can't just keep me here, he'll come looking for me. Can I at least have my clothes back... and a blanket? Wait, before you go, what time is it?"

Kade kept talking, but didn't receive a response. The leader and his minions exited the cell and shut the thick metal door, sealing Kade inside. Once again the room was swallowed by darkness.

Chapter Seventeen

Kade was in rough shape. Each passing hour felt like it could be his last. While he was still able to breathe, he didn't have any food, water, or clothing.

Coming down from his high, he had gone from a state of euphoria to feel like his brain was mud. He felt death would be an easier route than having to experience the crippling withdrawal symptoms and impending torture he was likely to face.

Despite the body shakes, aches, and hunger pangs, Kade eventually managed to drift off and catch up on some much needed sleep. After several hours, he was awoken once again by the sound of footsteps. By his estimation, it must have been late into the night or early morning at this point. It was hard to tell.

The door opened, but instead of a towering figure, he saw the slender silhouette of a woman standing in the doorway.

"Come on, get up," the female voice spoke. "I'm getting you out of here."

Kade wasn't sure if he was dreaming. He needed time to allow his brain to process what was happening.

"Unless of course you want to stay here?" the woman said.

"Who are you?" Kade said.

"Really? Am I that forgettable?" the woman said.

He recognized the voice. "You came back."

"So you do remember. The name is Cali."

"Why?"

"You'll have to ask my parents."

"No, not that. Why are you helping me?"

"I'm still trying to answer that question myself. Let's call it guilty conscience mixed with a hatred for those scavie scum."

Kade hesitated a moment, having serious reservations on whether or not he could trust her. He wanted to know more about this mysterious underground society and the kinds of horrible things that went on there. However, given the circumstances, any question he could come up with seemed moot, and given time was not on their side, he looked at her and stood up. As he did, he bared his full nudity to Cali.

"Whoa, slow down buddy, we hardly know each other."

Kade looked down almost completely oblivious that he was naked, then covered himself with his hands.

"Here, you can wrap yourself in this until we find your clothes. They're most likely with your bike, which is down the hall. I recognized it the second I saw it."

"I'm surprised you didn't try to steal it again," Kade said.

"That was one time! Gosh, you're never going to let me live that down, are you?"

The two exited the small cell and ran through the labyrinth of passageways that stretched out in all directions. The scavies had laid claim to this once abandoned and forgotten city and made an intricate network of underground tunnels that connected many of the buildings in the city.

"Seriously, I have to know. Why did you come back?" Kade asked.

"You sound surprised?" Cali said.

"I mean, based on what I know of you, you don't seem like the type."

"The type to come back and rescue someone."

"Yeah."

"Well, here I am, so I'm not sure what to tell you. Maybe your kindness rubbed off on me."

"Or maybe you're working an angle."

"Dude, you literally don't have anything. What could I possibly want from you?"

"Alright, sorry."

"Okay, look. I didn't come back for you. I came back for me. They captured me two years ago, held me against my will, and did unspeakable things to me. They broke me and tried to turn me into one of them — scavie scum. But I was never one of them. I was just biding my time, waiting for my moment to strike or escape. I tried to run yesterday, but... you saw how that turned out. Damn near died and I hadn't even made it ten kilometres. So I came back to figure out a new plan. They don't know that I tried to escape. But then I saw your bike and knew they had you. Trust me, you don't want to go through the hell that I went through. They'll break you too until you submit to them. They'll provide food, clothing, shelter, and that precious life liquid known as oxygen. In return, you have to be their ride-or-die soldier."

"A den of thieves," Kade commented, knowing their reputation.

"They're certainly not known for their charity work."

"Not for nothing, I appreciate you getting me out of here," Kade said sincerely

"Like I said, I'm not helping you, I'm helping myself. There's only one person in this world who cares about me, and you're looking at her. I'm going to get us out of here, but I need that sweet bike of yours."

"Hey, what time is it?" Kade asked.

"Are you being serious?"

"Yeah."

"It's 3:30 a.m. Why?"

"No reason," Kade said.

"You have somewhere to be? An appointment?"

"No, not exactly."

"Then what is it?"

"Why do you have to be such a ball buster?"

Cali turned around and motioned as if she were going to kick him in the groin, which caused Kade to flinch. Cali started laughing and then said, "I'm a ball buster to keep you on your toes. To keep you honest. If you're honest with me, then I'll be honest with you."

"Oh right, honest like the time you zapped me and took off with my bike?" Kade said.

"Man, you are so hung up on the past," she said as she continued to lead the way. "We were getting along so nicely, why did you have to ruin it?"

"You're a strange gal, you know that?"

"I do know that," she replied. "A strange gal who's saving your life."

Chapter Eighteen

In the early morning hours, Cali led Kade to find some clothing, not just to cover himself, but to blend in. Entering the locker room of an abandoned high school, Kade felt a sense of nostalgia. There were wood benches, metal cage lockers, and a faded Cougars mural still visible on the cinder block wall. In each of the lockers hung stale fabric that smelled just as bad as they looked.

"Here, put these on," Cali said, tossing Kade some scavie garb.

"Are you going to turn around?"

"Why, it's nothing I haven't seen before."

"Whatever."

Kade dropped his towel and began to layer himself with the torn rags. The cloth draped off him and he looked every bit the part of a scavie.

"Your face too," Cali said.

"You want me to cover my mouth with this disgusting rag? Who knows where this has been?"

"Unless you want to get caught, I suggest you get over your fear of odours and wrap that cloth around your face."

As much as Kade wanted to disagree, Cali had a point. He reluctantly covered his face with the cloth and began to breath.

"See it isn't so bad," Cali said with a smirk.

"It's worse than I thought. I think this part of the fabric used to cover someone's armpit."

"Ah, no wonder, you put it on upside down. That's the loincloth."

Kade immediately unraveled the cloth and gasped for air. Cali couldn't help but laugh. Kade balled up a mouthful of saliva and spit it on the floor.

Still amused, Cali confessed that she was just messing with him. "Come on, wrap up. We have to go."

"Where are we going?"

"To get your bike."

When they exited the locker room, something caught Kade's attention.

"Whoa, what's that?" he asked. His attention was fixed on the pool area.

"Oh, that's the tree farm. It's how we get our oxygen."

"Let's check it out."

"We don't have time," Cali insisted.

"It'll just be a sec."

Walking toward the pool room, Kade's eyes darted around trying to take in everything. The Olympic-sized pool was emptied of water and filled with dirt. Inside was a small forest of trees and other plant life. The entire thing was covered in plastic from the floor to the ceiling, which stretched up over fifty feet. Mounted on the ceiling were several large hydroponic lights that lit up the otherwise dark room. Cables and tubes snaked around strange equipment that connected from the indoor greenhouse to several large tanks.

"Oxygen comes in, gets funnelled through these tubes, and then goes into those tanks."

"It's incredible," Kade said in awe.

"I've been here so long that I take it for granted."

"I've heard about these tree farms, but I've never seen one before."

"We have several of these all over town. This is actually one of the smaller ones. We have one that takes up an entire warehouse. In fact, we have several of those."

"You guys must be rich. Why then do you resort to a life of petty crime?"

"Robbing people is more of a pastime. Not too many are foolish enough to come to these parts alone. No offense."

"None taken."

"We should go. Come on, follow me."

Cali rushed out of the pool area and down a series of halls. Kade tried his best to keep up, but his body was badly bruised. Each step made him wince in pain.

Cali and Kade entered the gymnasium, which had been converted into an equipment room. There were tables full of weapons and gear, with tools and parts scattered every which way. It looked like a messy mechanic shop crossed with a junkyard. Amid all the scrap metal, machinery, and salvaged cars was Kade's bike.

"I remember seeing it somewhere," Cali said in a whisper. "Unless they moved it."

"We should split up," Kade suggested in the same hushed tone.

"No, we stick together."

Together they moved silently through the heap, using on the faintest of morning light coming through the window to guide their way.

Navigating through the equipment room was challenging. There were a lot of things to bump into and alert someone of their presence. As Kade passed by a tool bench, he picked up a knife and tucked it under his robe.

"Is that it over there?" Cali asked.

"It's tough to say," Kade said, craning his neck. The jet-black bike was difficult to spot, but they made their way toward it. Just then, Kade's robe snagged a tool from one of the tables and dragged it to the floor. The large piece of metal smashed to the ground, creating a loud ruckus that echoed throughout the gym.

Cali spun around and glared at Kade with a stunned look. There was fear in her eyes, which was something Kade had never seen on her before. This in turn caused him to be even more concerned.

"We need to go now!" Cali said.

Chapter Nineteen

Large overhanging lights came on in succession, illuminating the repurposed gymnasium. Kade and Cali were not completely exposed. There was no place to run or hide. Before they knew it, they were surrounded by scavs.

Although Cali had rescued Kade, he didn't feel beholden to continue to help her. He ran to his bike, but couldn't find his helmet or suit anywhere. Without all his gear, there was no point in trying to escape. He needed everything if he were to survive the harsh environment.

Kade looked around frantically, but eventually was forced to pay attention to more pressing matters. He was attacked from the rear by two men, one of which had a large metal pipe. Luckily he saw the attack coming just in time to avoid a wild swing that, if it had connected, would have been life altering.

"If you help me get my gear, I can take you with me," Kade pleaded in a passive attempt to mollify the situation.

He figured Cali couldn't be the only unhappy person living against their will. Neither of the men took the offer.

Kade wasn't much of a fighter, but he was scrappy. In his line of work, he was no stranger to hand-to-hand combat. Even still, he was in no position or mood to fight. His body was badly beaten and his brain was fried. The Chu philosophy ran through his mind once again — increase the odds in your favour. Kade figured his best course of action was to run. He maneouvered himself behind a table, thinking that would prevent the attackers from getting him. The scavs simply jumped onto the table, forcing Kade to quickly come up with a new plan.

Cali was a warrior. She was dealing with even more scavs. They attacked her from all angles, but her clever and crafty movement always seemed to be one step ahead. While dodging a punch from one of the attackers, she spun around with the fluidity of a ballerina and kicked another in the face. Then in a dizzying flurry, she smashed kneecaps, obliterated noses, and sent ill intended kicks to groins. Within seconds, she had dismantled several of her attackers. Before she had a chance to help out Kade, there were a dozen more men coming from all directions.

Kade on the other hand had problems of his own. Cornered by two men, they traded blows. One of the men hit him with a taser, which dropped Kade to his knees. Then, another scav, a large fellow, hoisted Kade onto his shoulders like he was carrying a bag of rice, and slammed his body down on a table, forcing the air out of his lungs. Kade moaned in pain and struggled to get free, but one of his arms were pinned.

He looked over at his right arm, which was stretched out and being held in place by a man who outweighed him by nearly one hundred pounds. Kade's eyes cascaded up and saw the man holding a large machete high over his head. In his mind, Kade made the logical connection. If he didn't get out of this compromising position, he was about to lose an arm.

As the blade swung down, Kade withdrew a small knife from his robe and jabbed it into the man's leg. The machete slammed down on the table, inches away from dismembering a limb. As the man dealt with the knife in his leg, Kade slid off the table and limped away. He looked for another weapon and found a hammer. He held it out in a defensive stance, his eyes darting back and forth between the two men. He had a crazed look in his eyes that was a mixture of fear and panic.

One of the men charged forward in a flash, covering the distance between them with one stride. Before Kade could even swing, the man landed a solid punch squarely on his jaw. Kade was wobbled from the blow and could barely see straight. As he searched for his bearings, he was tackled to the ground. The two men proceeded to pummel him with a rage unlike anything he had seen. All Kade could do to protect himself was turtle up and hope they would grow tired.

The punches seemed never-ending as fists rained down on him, smashing into the meaty part of his already tender legs, rib cage, and arms, which were cradling his head. The odd punch managed to sneak through his defense and smash his face.

He had nothing left and was ready to submit. Then, a firestorm of gunshots echoed throughout the gymnasium. Kade prayed that none of the bullets would hit him. When the gunfire stopped, he opened his eyes and peaked through his arms. He saw his two attackers bloodied and deceased on the floor beside him. He looked over and saw Cali sitting on his bike. The guns had been withdrawn and had taken out everyone in the vicinity.

"I found your helmet," she said, looking like a total badass. "Come on, get up."

Chapter Twenty

It took every ounce of will for Kade to pull himself off the floor and return to his feet, but he knew he would not likely live to see another sunrise if he didn't. With a severe limp, he hobbled toward Cali.

"Can I have my helmet?" he asked as blood oozed from his nose as well as the corners of his mouth.

"Later," she replied. "Get on the back."

Kade removed a mask from one of the scavs before climbing on the back of the bike. As soon as he did, Cali took off, weaving through the field of debris. Kade quickly wrapped his arms around Cali's waist and held on tightly. He could feel her tight abs flex as she jockeyed around the large room. She had demonstrated admirable skill in both combat and riding, which intrigued him. He had to know more about her.

"Who are you?" he asked.

"Seriously, dude, not the right time to be asking questions," she shot back. Her focus was on getting them out alive.

With Kade clinging on, Cali accelerated through the rubble and out the nearest exit. They made their way to the street just as the hazy orange sun began to rise. They were still not out of danger yet, but fortunately, Cali knew exactly which way wasn't riddled with traps.

She shifted her weight like a pro as she raced through the empty streets. Around her shoulder was a large blaster. Gripping it with one hand, she spun the strap around and aimed the gun high letting out a succession of blasts. Kade didn't even see the target, but Cali knew all the hiding spots like going through a previously completed level of a video game. She took aim, blasting her enemies while navigating the streets.

Their clothes flapped with force as they tucked their heads and flew through the city, making it to the highway. They were home free. The rode for more than an hour, being sure to check over their shoulders every so often. They were not being followed.

In the middle of nowhere, several hundred kilometres outside of the city, Cali slowed the bike as she pulled into the temporary rest stop. Kade lifted his head and saw a little building with nothing else around it. Whatever township this once was, it had been wiped off the map and all that was left was a small stone structure.

The two dismounted and took turns rehydrating. Fortunately, the bike's water reservoir as nearly full.

"You're a good rider," Kade said.

"Thanks."

"Where are we?"

"A rest stop."

"What's the plan after this?" Kade asked, looking around the abandoned shelter.

"Let's worry about that later. First, we need to make sure we're both safe and in good health. How are you feeling? Anything broken?"

"I don't think so. A lot of swelling. My whole body is sore, but I think I'll pull through. I think I just need to lie down and allow my body to rest and heal up."

"I'm sorry to keep asking you this, but I have trust issues," Kade said. "I just don't understand why you're helping me? You didn't need me to escape. You have the bike and the helmet, you could have left me back there."

"Kind of like how you left me to die out in the desert?"

"Exactly."

"Well, fortunately I'm not like you," Cali said "I have a heart."

"I have a heart," Kade replied in defense.

"I know, and it just about got you killed."

"For the record, I knew you were trouble when I met you," Kade said.

"What made you turn around for me then?"

"Honestly, I heard my mother's voice. Not in a crazy way. It's just... before I left, we saw this young girl being attacked, and my mum insisted that I help her. I figured helping you might be good karma for my journey."

"Good karma for your journey? That's the dumbest thing I've ever heard."

"Alright, whatever, it worked didn't it?" Kade shot back.

"You're the first person I've talked to in years who has a heart," Cali said. "The world needs more of that."

"The second I helped you back in the desert, you zapped me and took off with my bike."

"And obviously you're still not over it. This is now the hundredth time you brought it up. Look, I'm not saying be like me. I'm not perfect. I guess... I don't know, you make me want to be a better person, you know? Before all this craziness happened with the world, human civilization was in a good place. For the most part, we were kind, we cared for one another. Now look at us. Everyone's living in a constant state of fear. Always looking over their shoulder, waiting for someone to stab them in the back. I was forced into a world of being one of those scavie scum and I needed to reclaim a sense of my humanity. I hated who I was becoming."

"There are still good people in the world. You can be the change you want to see."

"Okay, Ghandi."

"For what it's worth, I appreciate you saving me back there," Kade said.

"Don't mention it."

"So where did you learn to fight like that, and ride?"

"My mother," Cali said with a sense of sorrow.

"Was she a rider?"

"Not really, but she was sort of a master of whatever skill she wanted to pick up."

"Sounds like an incredible lady. Is she still alive?"

"I don't know."

"What about your father?"

"What about him?"

"Where is he?"

"I don't know, dude, what is this, a therapy session?"

"And the walls go up," Kade said. "Geez, you don't have to be so guarded all the time. I'm trying to connect with you."

"We can exchange backstories later, right now we need a plan," Cali said, eager to change the subject.

"Okay, fine. So what's your plan?" Kade asked.

"There's a saying I heard once that described travelling with a flashlight. It said even though you can only see ten feet in front of you, you can make the whole journey that way. So for me, I'm only looking ten feet ahead of me. Step one was to escape. Step two was to make it to some sort of functioning society. After that, it's anybody's guess where I go from there."

Kade didn't respond. There was a long moment of silence before Cali said, "Okay, you first."

"Me first, what?"

"Tell me about yourself — where are you from, what was your life like, do you have anyone who cares for you back home?"

"Not much to tell," Kade said, reflecting on his life. "Former junkie, rider, friend, son. I live alone with my dog Digi."

"Both parents still alive?"

"Just my mother."

"What happened to your father if you don't mind me asking."

"He was... helping people. He died a hero," Kade paused. Cali could see that he was choking up and holding back a lot of pain.

"Do you remember where you were when it happened?"

"I was 10, riding my bike in front of our house. I remember this big explosion and the ground shook. At first, I thought I had caused it after doing one of my tricks. I immediately looked at my mother, who was outside with me. She was looking up toward the sky. That's when I turned around and looked. The sky was being swallowed by a thick black cloud. From that day forward, things were never the same. It's funny to think of how much we take for granted, you know? Rarely do we stop to think, this will be the last time I see a blue sky, or a sunset... or see my father."

Kade's shoulders slumped as he put his head in his arms and sobbed.

"It's okay," Cali said. "You're a really good person. If you're dad is looking down on you, I know he would be proud of you."

Kade exhaled deeply to let his emotions decompress. "Sorry about that."

"What are you, Canadian? You have to stop apologizing for everything. You never have to apologize for getting emotional. This situation we're in... it happened to all of us. We all lost something that day."

"I was six years old, so I don't remember much. I only remember small glimpses of my childhood, but how much of that is my actual memory, or me just remembering what people told me?"

"Or that your brain made up. Memories can be very deceitful."

"Very true," Cali conceded. "I'll tell you what I think happened. Like I said, I was six years old. I was the eldest of three siblings. I had a younger brother and a younger sister. My parents were still together, but I don't necessarily think they were happy. We weren't exactly well off, so there was a lot of financial struggle, which caused a lot of tension. I remember seeing my parents fight a lot.

"My parents ran a restaurant and were barely scraping by. They had three young kids, my mother and aunt mostly looked after us while my dad was working to provide for the family. Then the volcano erupted and the business immediately shutdown. From what I'm told, things were pretty chaotic for a while, but at least we were alive. We were considered among the lucky ones.

"To make matters worse, my father accepted a job as part of the cleanup crew. I think a lot of people took that job. Two years later, he had developed lung cancer and died."

"I'm sorry to hear that," Kade said.

"I barely remember him at all. My only memories are from photographs. I don't even know what his voice sounded like or how he smelled.

"After my father passed, my mother did what she had to do to survive, which she didn't talk about, but as I got older I assumed the worst. What does a single mother with three kids do to provide? The most obvious answer is prostitution... she was hanging out with the wrong crowd and got hooked on ghost. She was dead in less than a year."

"I'm sorry, that must have been really difficult for your and your siblings."

"It's okay, I've made my peace with it," Cali replied without as much as shedding a tear. I was so young when it happened so it doesn't feel as though I lost anything. It's the only life I know. The other thing is, I don't blame anyone. It's no one's fault. It's neither good nor bad, it's just what happened. It is what it is. I'm twenty-four now and about the age that my mum was when she was raising three kids with no support. She was a fighter and I respect her for making difficult choices in difficult times."

"So what happened next?"

"Trust me, you don't want to know what happens to an eleven year old girl living on the streets by herself, especially in this world. But what I can tell you is that you tend to grow up fast, learn to be guarded, and not trust people. I'm incredibly selfish and don't know if I can ever find love or happiness. In fact, most days I don't even allow myself to feel sadness or pity. It's a messed up world and there's no room for weakness. I used to think showing emotion was a weakness, but as I get older and become more introspective, I realize that to be emotional is to be human. If we all showed more of our humanity to each other, this world would be a better place. I truly believe that."

"You're brother and sister?" Kade asked. "Are they still around?"

"I have no idea where they are or if they're alive. I like to think they're out there, somewhere, hopefully doing better than me. I think about them from time to time and wonder if they even remember me."

"I'm sure they do," Kade said in an effort to comfort.

"You're lucky that you have your mother," Cali said.

"Actually, I'm not sure my mother is still around," Kade said, bowing his head remorsefully. "She was taken by my employer and held as ransom. He said if I don't complete this mission, then... well, you can guess what will happen to her."

"Are you being serious? That is so messed up. I mean, if it was me..." Cali stopped herself. "Actually, you know what... that is me. I basically work for a guy who took everything from me."

"Then I guess we have something in common," Kade said. "We do what we do to survive."

"Do you ever think about killing him?"

Kade chuckled then looked Cali straight in the eye and said, "Every day."

"So why don't you? Wouldn't that solve a lot of your problems?"

"First of all, I'm not a killer. Second, even if I were, killing Saigon would be much easier said than done. Third... you ever hear the saying, you never bite the hand that feeds you? If I kill Saigon, I lose my main employer. Then my problems only get worse. That's assuming I get away with it, which I probably won't. But if I did, and that's a big 'if', I no longer have a steady source of income."

"Are you doing a delivery for him right now?"

Kade had major trust issues and reservations about opening up to a stranger, but he seemed to be bonding with Cali.

"Yeah, I have two more days to get a package to Tri-City and the clock is ticking. If I don't then my mother is dead, and when I return, he'll probably kill me along with everyone I know. That would be getting off lightly. He'll most likely torture me first, which won't be pleasant. In that situation, I assure you, death would be a blessing."

"What's in the package?"

"I have no idea."

"You're going all this way, risking your life, and you have no idea what you're delivering?"

"I never look. It's against my code of ethics."

Cali burst out laughing, unable to contain herself. "Code of ethics," she repeated, still having a chuckle. "That's funny."

"Why is that so funny?"

"You're living in a dystopian wasteland where civilization is clinging to survival. It's basically a matter of time before we all die of some horrible catastrophe or from killing each other. There's no such thing as a code of ethics. It's all about survival. You do what you have to do to survive. That's it."

"What happened to all that talk about having a heart and showing more of our humanity to one another? You said I make you want to be a better person. You seem very conflicted, Cali. I think you want to be good, but you don't know how. You have these moments of good, but then you put this wall up, and your hardened jaded side comes roaring back. I think deep down, we're all good. You rescued me because it was the right thing to do, which is a code of ethics that is still deep within you."

"Save your philosophy for someone else. I look out for me. That's my only code of ethics."

"I don't believe that. I think those are just your walls coming up, trying to protect you. It's your instinct. It's all you've ever known. Trust doesn't happen overnight, but I see good in you, Cali. I hope you see it in yourself. I'm going to go out on a limb and say that I trust you."

"I hope you don't feel bad when I double-cross you."

"I believe in the good of all people and you won't double-cross me."

"Okay. Tell that to your man who killed your mother and will kill you and everyone you know if you don't do what he says. Is there good in him?"

"I believe so, he's just lost his way. If society is going to change, it must start with the individual."

Again, Cali laughed in a mocking tone. "Look, I appreciate your idealistic viewpoint of the world, but I have to get some sleep."

"Goodnight, Cali," Kade said sincerely.

"Whatever."

Chapter Twenty-One

In the morning, Kade awoke with a splitting headache and dark rings around his eyes. He was on death's doorstep. Still feeling withdrawal symptoms from the ghost, each day was worse than the previous as his body craved the drug. The cold sweats and shakes were so severe that he was unable to get a proper night's rest, which only exacerbated his feeling of depletion.

As Kade attempted to stand, every bone and muscle in his body ached. Once on his feet, his brain started piecing together the events that led him to being where he was. He looked around at the four walls that surrounded him and saw that he was inside a tiny stone structure — a destroyed church that had been abandoned long ago. He didn't see Cali anywhere. He looked down and saw a taser, most likely left for him. It had been placed there at some point after he had gone to sleep.

Kade contorted his back to stretch out the tight knots that was a result of a lifetime of riding, mixed with sleeping on unforgiving floors. He went outside to look for Cali. Stepping out of the tiny church, he was met with nothing but the wind and the warm rays of the hidden sun. In every direction was endless landscape of dirt and rocks bathed in an orange haze. There were no trees, flowers, or weeds as far as the eye could see. A once lush and vibrant forest was now a wasteland that resembled the surface of Mars more than Earth.

Cali was gone, and she had taken the bike. There was no sign of her anywhere, not even her tread marks to indicate which direction she had gone. The wind had since covered those. A part of him wasn't upset with Cali. She had warned him not to trust her.

Listening to the whistling wind he realized he was the only living organism within a hundred kilometres. He tapped the side of his helmet to bring up the display to check the temperature, his bio-stats, and most importantly, his oxygen levels. Another quick tap and the display disappeared.

Returning to the tiny shack, he wanted to get out of the sun and rest, partly to heal his body but also to conserve his oxygen. His only option was to hope and pray for a miracle, which in this life, wasn't worth waiting for. Laying down on hard floor, he took those moments of quiet contemplation to think about his life and the choices he had made up until that point.

With no food or water, no transportation, no eco-suit, and limited oxygen supply, he knew this would likely be his final place of rest. He had come to terms with death, but wasn't looking forward to the slow agonizing decent of starvation and dehydration. If there were any kind of consolation, it was that he would no longer have to deal with Saigon ever again.

He thought about his mother and whether or not she was still alive. He then weighed out the possible scenarios. If he were to somehow make it out of this situation and return to Endocrine without the package, Saigon would surely kill him. Although, there may be some small chance Saigon would spare his life, as unlikely as that may seem. However, the package was with the drone on some random rooftop in the abandoned city, and it would be impossible to find without his helmet, which he didn't have. Even if he did have it, going back into scav territory was just as much of a death wish as baking out in the hot sun and waiting for dehydration to kill him. Either way, he was in a lose-lose situation.

With each passing hour, his condition worsened. He was still clinging to a glimmer of hope that Cali would return for him. Perhaps it was a prank she was playing on him, or maybe she just went out to look for food and water and she got lost, or her bike broke down, or she got captured. After spending half the day with nothing but his thoughts, he came to the sad conclusion that she was not coming back. She had left him to die.

Kade picked up the taser and thought about using it to kill himself. For the next four hours he weighed out all the pros and cons until he decided that it would be the best course of action to take. There was nothing left to live for and no point in delaying the inevitable.

He took one last moment to briefly reevaluate his decision, and then slowly raised the taser to his throat and held it there. A tear rolled down his face as he was seconds away from taking his last breath and leaving this cruel world. Thoughts of his mother came flooding in, which overwhelmed his emotions. His hands started to tremble as the intensity of the sobbing increased. Tears soaked his glossy cheeks, his eyes squeezed tightly shut. This was it, his final moment. Thoughts of despair competed with thoughts about his sweet mother who had nurtured him and protected him since he was a baby. She would never see her son's face again, and he would never see hers, at least not in this life, but perhaps in the next. Thinking about her was gut wrenching.

"I'll see you on the other side, ma. Please forgive me. I love you."

Kade squeezed the trigger of the taser. In a flash, 50,000 volts of electricity surged through his body, causing his muscles to clamp down on the trigger and stiffen. He gritted his teeth and kept holding the taser as long as he could until his brain shut off. A moment after he had began, his arm went limp and he dropped the taser. He now lay motionless on the floor, his eyes closed, and gone from this wasteland of a planet called Earth.

Chapter Twenty-Two

"What's happening, mama?" a young boy asked his mother.

Kade sensed his mother's panic and quickly peddled toward the open garage.

"I'm not sure, but we need to get inside now."

"What about papa? Is he going to be okay?"

"Your father is going to be just fine. I'll call him now."

Kade's mother turned on the news and saw live feeds of the disaster. The Caldera supervolcano located Yellowstone National Park had erupted and was spewing hot lava hundreds of feet in the air. Scientists were being interviewed on television, speaking about the long-term environmental, economic, and social impacts.

"We are entering the early stages of another mass extinction event," one scientist said. "This will come in several waves that people need to prepare for.

"The first wave to hit us will be infrastructure breakdown. Roads will become congested, making it difficult to mobilize and have first-responders come to people's aid. Delivery drivers won't be able to supply food, medicine, and other essential items to distributors. Hospitals will be overwhelmed and unable to treat those in need. People will not receive proper food, water, and medical care.

"This will lead to the second wave, which is a complete collapse of society. Riots, looting, murder will all become common place as systems erode and people become desperate.

"Next will be a widespread famine. Crop yields will plummet, millions of people living in cities will die of starvation.

"The fourth wave will hit whoever remains in rural environments. Pestilence brought on by a lack of clean drinking water and sewage treatment will wipe out nearly everyone.

"The final wave will be from a lack of oxygen. After the trees and plant life die off, people will simply suffocate to death.

"There will be survivors, but they will be few. To quote Thomas Hobbes, life on Earth will be nasty, brutish, and short. Ninety-nine point nine percent of all life on this planet will eventually die within ten to fifteen years.

"Over time, hundreds of thousands or millions of years, Earth will undergo cataclysmic shifts in climate and other environmental changes. The sky will eventually return to its natural state, and a new life will begin again.

"It goes in cycles," the scientist said frankly. "The dinosaurs were around a lot longer than us and they became extinct. Now it is our turn. We had our run. It was a good run. And we will leave this planet for the next civilization that comes after us. By then, nothing man made, aside from large stone structures will remain.

"The next intelligent life that comes after us will think they're the first. They will postulate about the stars as we once did, they will develop philosophy and mathematics, science and medicine, they will have inventions and discoveries, and a life they call their own. It may look nothing like our civilization, or it may be pretty similar.

"As a scientist, I can say with confidence there's nothing we can do to prevent this from happening. I recommend gathering all your family and friends, enjoy each other as much as possible, and hope that you die quickly."

The matter of factness in which the scientist spoke was enough to freak anyone out. Kade's mother stared at the screen holding her mouth open in shock. Her eyes welled up with sadness as despair set in.

***

Kade's body was in transit. A group of insurgents had found him up and where carting him back to their base — a dwelling carved into the mountains. His body had endured a beating and had succumb to a comatose state in an effort to repair itself.

Kade's mask had been pulled off and replaced by one of their own. One of the insurgents — a former doctor — tended to Kade by injecting him with a dose of steroids and a sedative. A saline drip hung overhead, slowly delivering much needed fluids into his depleted body.

Chapter Twenty-Three

Morning came and went, and Kade was still unconscious. He remained asleep for nearly three days, being kept alive by a rogue group of mountain people. When he began to show signs of life, the doctor was called to his side. Kade's eyes opened and he was in a profound state of confusion. He didn't recognize his surroundings, nor the faces staring over him.

"It's okay," the doctor said, "My name is Kefu. You're in a safe place."

For a moment Kade considered the possibility that he may in fact be dead. The room he was in didn't exactly fit the traditional images of heaven so his brain quickly searched for another explanation.

"Where am I?" he muttered with a course voice. His throat was dry and scratchy. He coughed immediately, which caused him excruciating pain. Kefu handed him a glass of water with a metal straw, which Kade immediately slurped up.

"You're in a monastery," Kefu said. "My people found you several days ago and have been tending to you while you recover."

Kade had so many questions, but wasn't sure where to start. "Thank you," Kade said. The confused look never left his face. "How long did you say I have been here?"

"We found you three days ago."

"Three days ago?" Kade said, nearly falling out of his bed.

"Please, you must relax. Your body needs to rest."

"Was there a girl with me?" Kade asked. "About 5'5", light brown hair, mid-twenties."

"No, you were alone when we found you. It appears as though someone brought you to a very fortunate spot. We didn't find any transportation so we assumed you had been beaten and left for dead. You did have a taser lying next to you so whoever left you, didn't think to disarm you. A friend perhaps."

"Cali is no friend of mine."

"Did you say, 'Cali'?" the monk asked in astonishment.

"Yeah, why, did she betray you as well?"

"Mr..."

"Casey. Kade Casey. You can call me Kade."

"Very well, Kade. I'm not too sure your circumstances and what your relationship with Cali was, but I can assure you, she has a big heart."

"Ha!" Kade scoffed, followed by another coughing fit. "We must be talking about two different people. She robbed me and left me for dead. Twice."

"How did she do that?" the monk asked.

"We were in the abandoned city and she helped me escape. Then she took my bike and all my equipment and left me for dead."

"If what you say is true, why did she help you escape?"

"I'm not sure."

"Was there some benefit she gained in doing so?"

"I'm not sure."

"Well, I know Cali. She helped us out a great deal a few years back. Haven't seen her since. If it wasn't for her, this community wouldn't exist, we'd all be slaves or dead. I don't think it was an accident that she left you where she did. She knows very well that the building you were in is used as a lookout post. We go there often. She knew you would eventually be discovered and provided assistance. The fact that she left you with a weapon and a near full canister is evidence of that. If she were truly out to get you, she would have left you with nothing."

"Maybe so, but it doesn't change the fact that she stole my gear."

"I cannot condone what she did, nor speculate on the reasons for her actions, but perhaps in time, her true motives will be revealed."

"I appreciate you rescuing me, but I can't stay here. I need to get back to Endocrine."

"That is a journey few can survive, especially one in your condition."

"Thanks for the advice, but there's something I really need to take care of."

"I suggest you stay here and rest. We can provide you with food, clothing, oxygen, safety, and shelter. In exchange, we ask you help out. Within a week or two, your body will have recovered adequately and we can give you all the supplies you need to go on your journey."

"A week or two?" Kade repeated. "I cannot wait that long. I need to leave immediately."

As Kade attempted to stand, sharp pains pulsed through his body. He gritted his teeth and squinted his eyes in discomfort.

"You are free to go anytime, you're not a prisoner here,"
the monk said. "But if you would like to stay, we can ensure
you make a full recovery."

Chapter Twenty-Four

Drifting in and out throughout the night, Kade tossed and turned in his sweat-soaked sheets, moaning loudly like he was exercising a demon from his body. His body fluctuated from having a high fever to having cold sweats as he was desperately craving another hit of ghost. On more than one occasion the thought had crossed his mind to sneak out, find his way back to the abandoned city, and locate the dose he had thrown away. He played out the sequence in his mind over and over like an obsessed madman, minimizing the amount of effort and luck it would take.

Kefu came in several times throughout the night to check on him.

"Mr. Kade, can I get you anything?"

"Water. Please."

Kefu stepped away and returned a moment later with a glass filled with a dark brown liquid.

"Here, drink this."

Kade accepted the drink and brought it up to his nose.

"What is this?"

"It's medicine," Kefu said with a warm smile. "It'll make you feel better."

If the drink tasted anything like it smelled, Kade knew he wouldn't enjoy it. He started with a small sip and nearly gagged, not trying to conceal his disgust. He took another sip.

"Drink up," Kefu said, "I'll get you new bedding."

As he did with the water, Kefu shuffled off and returned yet again to help Kade through the ordeal.

As he changed the bedding, Kade explained his situation and why he was having withdrawal.

"I'm not a junkie, I promise," Kade said. "I was drugged."

"I don't pass judgement," Kefu said with the warm smile. "There, all done. Enjoy your new sheets. I'll be back in a few hours to check on you."

"What would I do without you, Kefu?" Kade said sincerely.

"It's important you get rest."

Kade smiled and shut his eyes.

"I'll wait with you until you fall asleep," Kefu said.

"Thank you," Kade said. "For everything."

It the morning, Kade awoke with a massive headache, brought on by extreme dehydration. His eyes slowly opened and he saw Kefu sitting bedside as if he had never left.

"Another drink for you," Kefu said, handing Kade another glass of the murky liquid.

Kade reluctantly accepted the strange brew and again choked it down. "What's in this?" he asked again, hoping to get a more specific answer.

"It's a concoction of fermented psilocybin mushrooms, tree bark, beetle protein, and mineral water."

"That explains the crazy dreams," Kade said with a smirk. "My morning should be interesting to say the least."

"Don't worry, I only used a small dose of mushrooms, you should hardly experience any psychedelic effects."

Kade took another sip.

"When you're ready, you can eat. We have breakfast prepared for you."

"Thank you."

Kefu stood up and went to leave until Kade stopped him. "Wait," Kade said causing Kefu to turn around.

"Yes?"

"Did you say tree bark?"

"Yes," he said, flashing his large smile.

"You have a tree here?"

"Of course, we have several. How do you think we're breathing right now?"

"Can I see them?"

"Yes, of course. After breakfast I will take you to our tree habitat."

Kade struggled to get out of bed as he was experiencing a combination of muscle fatigue, atrophy, and a debilitated mental state brought on by withdrawal.

"Don't try to walk," Kefu said, rushing to bring him a wheelchair.

Kade could barely stand. With Kefu's help, he was assisted into the chair and together, they entered a large eating area where Kade was met by over two dozen friendly faces, who were all eager to meet him. It wasn't often they had visitors, and consequently they received great joy from being of service to others.

Kefu wheeled Kade up to a table and locked his chair in place. A moment later, a large plate of steaming potatoes and boiled vegetables were placed in front of him.

"This looks amazing," he said graciously. "Thank you all for your warm hospitality."

"It's our pleasure," one of the monks responded.

"I'm Tenchu," an elegant woman said with an endearing smile. "What brings you to these parts?"

"I'm a rider... from Endocrine. I was just passing through on one of my deliveries, and... well, it didn't go as I had planned it."

"You are safe here."

"I appreciate it, thank you."

After breakfast, Kade was wheeled around the facility. He was shown the exercise and rehabilitation room, the medical centre, the sleeping bunks, and the entertainment area. The place was massive.

The monastery was a modern facility, formerly an abandoned military bunker carved into the side of a mountain. It was completely off the grid. Apparently, whoever knew about it before the catastrophe had either perished or had no interest in returning. Fortunately for the monks, it was fully stocked with everything they needed, including seeds, fertile soil, fresh water and oxygen, medical equipment, and food.

The monks had discovered the base by accident and had remained there ever since. The only encounter they had was with a group of scavs a few years prior, who upon finding it, threatened to take it over and kill everyone inside. Cali was among those scavs — a newcomer at that time — and could not allow her conscience to sit back and watch such a peaceful group be slaughtered.

Kefu saved the best for last. The last place on the tour was a large glass dome with plants and trees. Insects such as butterflies and beetles thrived in this lush habitat. It was truly spectacular to see in person. Above the trees were a series of reflective tubes that connected to the surface, bringing natural sunlight to the underground oasis.

"We are the guardians of this place," Kefu stated with pride. "This is our home."

"This is incredible," Kade said, looking around in awe. It was unlike anything he had ever seen in his lifetime. "Where did this come from?"

"It was here when we discovered this place — to some extent. We, of course, nurture and maintain it. This is where we get all our food and oxygen. Without it, this place would be uninhabitable. As you know, there are no signs of life anywhere around us, which is ironically one of the things that keeps us safe. No one thinks to come looking for anything out here. Even if a drone were to fly overhead, it wouldn't even detect this place. We have technology to mask our digital signals so unless you happen to stumble upon this place like we did, or are brought here like you were, we can remain completely off the grid and safe."

"It's truly a wonderful spot you have, nestled in the mountains, protected from being corrupted by the outside world. I'm really honoured to be here and have you take such good care of me."

"We'd be delighted for you to stay with us for as long as you want. This is home now."

"I appreciate that, but I mustn't stay too long. I need to return to Endocrine to see how my mother is doing. I've been given one week to make a delivery and I'm afraid I failed to deliver. My mother was being held as ransom. I need to tell my employer that I need more time."

"I'm terribly sorry to hear that," Kefu said. "I can assure you that we will help you in any way. If there's anything you need, it's yours."

"You're too kind," Kade said. "Thank you. The world needs more people like you."

Chapter Twenty-Five

Kade had spent the better part of a week at the monastery, first wheeling around, and then hobbling on crutches. He was trying to make himself as useful as possible, but also took adequate time to rest in bed, hoping his mind and body would heel.

His lack of mobility was frustrating. He needed to find a way to get back to Endocrine and see if his mother was still alive. It was not a life he wished to return to, but for his own sanctity, he needed to do everything in his power to save his mother and potentially others he was close to. He would surely be killed upon arrival, but there was a small chance that he would be spared and given another way to appease Mr. Saigon.

Kade sat humbly at a long table, eagerly anticipating his next meal. "Thank you," he said, accepting a plate of food. He immediately began shoveling potatoes and other vegetables in his mouth. Periodically, he would massage the back of his stiff neck.

After dinner, Kefu visited Kade in his room and checked his stats once again.

"Your body is recovering well," Kefu said.

"You take good care of me."

"It's more than just my care," Kefu said. "This seems to be the work of the divine."

"No offense, Kefu, but if there is a God, he gave up on this planet, and he certainly has abandoned me a long time ago. After the things I've seen and the places I've been, no benevolent God would allow this to happen."

"Maybe so, but who are we to question his or her authority and the divine plan. There are great benefits that are a result of great tragedy. Our scope of view is too narrow to understand broadly."

Kefu took the usual blood samples and checked Kade's vitals. "How is everything feeling?" Kefu asked. "Are there any nagging issues?"

"I didn't think to mention it before because my entire body was sore," Kade said, "but my neck is killing me."

"Oh?" Kefu said, taking a closer look. "What seems to be the problem?"

"I don't know," Kade said, massaging the back of his neck. "Sometimes I feel like slow dull ache, and other times I feel this sharp pain. It's almost as if someone is sticking a hot poker in the back of my neck."

"Okay, lean forward. I'll take a look."

Kefu placed a light above Kade and looked carefully at the back of his neck. "Hmm, this is unusual," he said.

"What is it?" Kade asked.

"There appears to be a small scar on the base of your hairline. I must have missed it before. What happens when I press down on it?" Kefu asked.

Just then, a sharp pain shot through Kade's body and he reared his head back. "Ow!" he hissed.

"I think I felt something under your skin. I would like to make a small incision and see if I can get it out," Kefu said.

"What do you think it is?" Kade asked.

"I'm not sure, a piece of shrapnel perhaps. Given your line of work, it could be any number of things. It looks fresh though. Have you been near any blasts lately?"

Kade laughed. "Every day someone is trying to kill me."

"Well, not today," Kefu said with a warm smile.

Kefu cleaned the area and injected Kade with a local anesthesia. He then picked up a scalpel and pressed it firmly against the skin. As he drew the blade down, it sunk into his soft flesh and left a small trail of blood in its wake. The slit was only a centimetre long, but that was large enough to extract whatever was burrowed inside.

"There it is," Kefu said, "Now, I'm just going to see if I can get it out..." his voice drifted off as he concentrated. Kefu pinched the surrounding skin like a pimple and a tiny metallic object poked out. Using a set of tweezers, Kefu carefully removed the object and rinsed it off in a nearby tray of water.

Kade couldn't feel a thing. He sat there patiently until Kefu was finished.

"All done," he said, placing the small object in a shallow metal container. "This is definitely not a piece of shrapnel."

Chapter Twenty-Six

Kade had stayed at the monastery a lot longer than he
had planned. Even though his body had recovered, he
thought the extra time with the monks would be good for
his mental state. It had been over three months since Kade
was brought to the monastery. He knew he couldn't stay
there indefinitely and the time had come to leave. With no
communication with the outside world, he had no idea if his
mother and Tanjoban were still alive, but he needed to get
back to Endocrine to find out. No more running. No more
hiding. He was ready to face his reality.

Equipped with a two-day supply of oxygen and a
motorbike that he had restored, Kade said his final goodbyes
to Kefu and the other monks.

"I am forever indebted to you," Kade said to Kefu, pulling
him in for a hug. If I can, I promise to make it back out this
way to repay you. If you don't hear from me, assume the
worst."

"We hope to see you again soon, Kade," Kefu said with his infectious smile. "Be safe out there."

Kade mounted his bike and descended down the steep mountainous road. The road was slick from a morning rain — the type of rain that wreaks havoc on anything it touches. He had to be careful to avoid puddles.

After three months off, it felt good to be riding again. Winding down the mountain, the bike's suspension and handling were put to the test. Once he reached the flats, he could really open up and see how fast it was. He had low expectations considering the age of the bike, the size of the motor, and what he had previously.

As the mountain road came to an end, Kade was heavy on the throttle. His equipment was basic and he had no navigational system other than the directions the monks had told him. He didn't have a drone, no weapons, and no high-tech suit. He needed to be careful and calculated about his every move.

He soon passed by the abandoned church in which he tried to take his own life, reminding him that it wasn't over until he breathed his last breath. He felt as though there was some higher force watching over him, guiding him.

An early morning fog crept in as Kade tucked his head and raced toward the abandoned city. His plan was to make it back to Endocrine, visit Mr. Saigon, and explain the situation. His hopes were that Saigon would give him another chance and spare his life. With any luck, his mother and Tanjoban would be safe as well.

It took a few hours until Kade approached the outer limits of the abandoned city. He needed a break, not only to stretch, but also to rehydrate. Success on this journey meant taking the right precautions. Mr. Chu's wisdom played in his head — 'You must stack the odds in your favour.'

Sitting at the edge of the city, Kade heard something in the distance. It wasn't coming from the city, it was coming from behind him. Kade turned to look. He had to squint through the thick orange haze to make out what it was. It appeared to be a small army charging toward him. Kade quickly mounted his bike and attempted to turn on the ignition, but it was dead.

"No no no, not now. Come on!" he said as he tried over and over to get the bike to start.

He got off the bike and fiddled with some wires that he believed may have been faulty. The whole time he kept looking at the swarming cavalry that was heading straight for him. His heart was racing.

When the large group punched through the fog and came within proper view, he realized the full scope of what he was dealing with. They weren't scavs at all, but something much more terrifying. The group was part human part machine — an unnerving sight for anyone especially a lone rider.

Upon his initial count, there appeared to be a dozen or so warriors with their makeshift Mad Maxian hell machines. Accompanying them were several unpiloted steampunk inspired bots that looked like they were assembled in a junkyard. Their haphazard metal plates, rusted mechanisms, and exposed gears were definitely not the work of refined engineers, but more the brainchild of a modern day Frankenstein.

Kade looked on in horror, his heart pounding violently as he kept fiddling with the outdated circuitry. Fear grew as he began yelling and hitting the bike out of a panic-stricken frustration. Just as the machines were within a stone's throw, the bike finally turned over and came to life. In one fluid movement, Kade revved the throttle and dove on the seat while the bike was in motion.

The bike accelerated as Kade climbed on properly and readjusted himself. On a straight stretch, he had a chance to turn his head back, but only for a glimmer, to see how close they were. They were right on his tail. He definitely didn't have the horsepower to outrun them, but he could definitely outride them. His skill as a rider was second to none and he had every bit of confidence that he would avoid capture by this rogue squad of bandits, whoever they were.

The machines came in all shapes and sizes, some resembling headless horses while others had tank treads. They were fast, calculated, and relentless. The slower ones took aim and fired off several rounds of explosive projectiles. The streets and surrounding buildings exploded with debris, narrowly missing Kade as he ducked his head and manoeuvered through the streets as if they were a mine field. Little rocks, pieces of metal, and chunks of concrete rained down on him and gummed up his visor. His visibility was so impaired that at one point he had to wipe the dirt away.

The bike howled through the vacant streets as he zigged and zagged around road hazards and large objects. He knew the streets were rigged by scavs, but wasn't exactly sure where all the traps were. That information would either help him or hurt him, but surely his pursuers would run into the same unexpected issues, putting them at a disadvantage.

Kade rounded a corner, but this time saw the cable stretched out. He propped himself up so that he was standing on the seat and waited for the exact moment to jump. As the bike passed under the steel cable, Kade timed it so that he jumped over it. He became separated from his bike for a second as he cleared the cable before crashing back down on the bike. The bike wobbled, but Kade quickly corrected and regained control.

He then realized there was another cable stretched out twenty feet away that was approaching rather quickly. It was positioned much too low to perform the same stunt, so he slammed on his front break causing the bike to do a nose wheelie. The bike wheeled right up to the cable, which is when Kade used his body momentum to swing the backend of the bike in the air and clear the cable. He then shifted his weight and pulled the front end up hopping over the cable like a choreographed dance.

Kade resettled the bike on the other side of the cable and took off. Rounding the next corner, he heard the moment of impact. The metal militia plowed into the first cable, snapping it upon impact. The gang hardly even noticed it.

Kade had no time to waste. He passed by one of the buildings he recognized and figured it was close to his drone and the package, but there was no time to look. The best-case scenario would be to find a place to hide and lay low.

The bots came from all angles, galloping like demons out of hell. They leaped over large objects in a single bound without breaking stride. They caught up to Kade and swiped at him, but he managed to out manoeuvre them. Kade sunk lower into his seat to remain a smaller target. Glancing over, he saw one of the bots charging toward him from the side. It plowed into him causing his bike to wobble uncontrollably. The handlebars jerked back and forth and Kade was thrown off his bike. He hit the dirt-covered ground with a thud and slid to a stop. In his wake was a large cloud of dust. His bike flipped end over end before crashing into a wall. It appeared to be completely destroyed. Kade winced in pain, but before he could move, he was surrounded.

The headless horse bot galloped toward him and with its solid frame, sharp edges, and imposing statue. It stood over Kade, pinning him to the ground.

Chapter Twenty-Seven

Kade hadn't made it very far in his journey before being captured once again. He was sure to be killed or enslaved by this race of warrior people. He struggled to get free, but it was no use - the heavy metallic bot had him pinned.

Within seconds, the rest of the squad showed up. A badass woman with war paint and makeshift armour stepped into his field of vision. From his perspective, she appeared to be eight feet tall as she towered over him. She shoved the barrel of her gun in his face.

"If you try to run, I will put a bullet in your head," the woman said.

Just then, the bot stepped aside allowing Kade to return to his feet. He was covered in dust and stood with a slightly bent leg that had been injured in the crash.

"Let's go," she said, still pointing her gun at him.

Kade was met by another woman, equally powerful in stature. He had yet to say a word. She grabbed his wrist and scanned him. "It's him," she notified the others.

Kade wasn't sure what that meant or even who these women were. They certainly didn't look like scavs. Some had long flowing hair that spilled out the backs of their helmets, while others kept it short. They were all equipped with state-of-the-art weapons, battle armour, and bots.

Their vehicles littered the street, with each driver holding a weapon on standby. If anything were to attack them, they'd be ready.

The woman holding Kade's wrist slapped a thick, metal cuff on him and connected it another cuff on the other wrist. With his arms now bound behind his back, he was escorted to one of the vehicles.

"Who are you people?" he asked. "What do you want with me?"

"We're bounty hunters," the lead woman said. "We're here to take you in."

"Take me in?" Kade said in confusion. "Who issued the bounty?"

Kade's question went unanswered, but he had an idea who would issue the bounty. In fact, he didn't exactly mind being captured. He was on his way to Endocrine to see Mr.

Saigon anyway, at least now he would have an armoured escort.

Kade was shoved into the back of a vehicle with force. He then heard the leader give a command to rally the squad to leave. The had got what they had come for. One by one, the metal militia pulled away leaving behind a large cloud of dust.

The all-women squad made their way through town, resembling a military convoy. There was an eerie presence that consumed them and kept them on high alert at all times. They knew they were not alone.

Kade was in the back of a dust-covered vehicle, unsure what his fate would be. He peered out and saw movement in one of the buildings. Scavs. He turned his head in the other direction and saw more of them. An ambush was coming and he was utterly defenseless. He wondered if he should say something or let it play out.

Before he had a chance to decide, shots were fired. A barrage of gunfire rained down from all angles.

"Spread out!" the leader shouted. The vehicles sped up, racing through the city, taking every direction possible. The bots followed closely behind, acting as their backup, firing back at targets they could not see. The scavs were prepared; this was their world. Every block had barricades and traps, along with vantage points to wage an attack.

The vehicles split up, making themselves even more vulnerable. The vehicle Kade was in picked up speed, fishtailing in the loose dirt. As it rounded a corner, it ran over a landmine that exploded under one of the front tires. The blast uprooted the vehicle, flipping it on its side. With a thunderous crash, it slammed into the ground and slid to a stop. Kade was still in the back, rattled, but alive. In the distance, he could hear the violent sounds of gunfire and explosions and realized getting to Endocrine would not be so easy.

Before the dust settled, Kade had scrambled out of the vehicle and belly crawled toward a hollowed out vehicle resting permanently on the side of the road. He struggled with his cuffs, but they were locked solid. He looked around to orient himself, but was completely mixed up. Having only spent a brief moment in the city, he had no idea where he was and what way he needed to go to escape.

Kade stayed put, lying on his back and listening to the sounds of scavs scurrying around him like rodents. They were communicating with each other through their interconnected network in their helmets, so he couldn't hear what they were saying. He inched forward for a better view, but remained low so that he wouldn't be spotted.

The large scav leader — the one who had come into Kade's cell one night — entered the street with a small crew. He walked right up to the flipped vehicle, knelt down, and looked inside. He said something to the wounded woman who was still inside.

Kade watched on with intrigue.

The scav reached inside the vehicle and dragged the warrior woman into the middle of the street. She kicked and fought with him, but had been weakened in the crash, so it wasn't much of a resistance. The leader scav then pulled out a gun and put it to her head.

Kade watched on and tried to ignore his moral compass, but almost uncontrollably, he stood up to reveal himself, "Don't shoot!" he pleaded.

Instantly, a dozen guns were aimed in his direction.

"Show me your hands," the scav said.

"I can't," Kade replied, turning around slowly to reveal his bound arms.

"Walk toward me," the scav leader said. "Slowly."

Kade did exactly as he was instructed and shuffled his feet toward the small scav army. "That's enough," the leader said, aiming his gun at him. "Who are you?"

With Kade's face concealed, the scav leader had no idea that Kade was the same person who was captured and escaped months prior.

"I'm nobody," Kade said. "Just a rogue traveller passing through until I was captured by these women."

"Why have you captured this man?" the scav leader asked.

"We're scavengers just like you. We take whatever may be of use to us," the warrior woman said, not revealing Kade's true identity. "We were just passing through," she said. "We mean you no harm."

Without warning, Kade's shackles unlocked and dropped to the ground with a thud. Kade looked just as stunned as anyone. The noise was just enough of a distraction to cause the scav leader to divert his attention away from the warrior woman. That's when she removed a blade from her belt and lunge forward, plunging it into the leader's ribs. Surprised by the attack, the leader fell forward, gasping for breath. He fell face first into the dirt. The warrior woman wasted no time. She quickly ran for cover, removing her weapon from its holster and began blasting.

In the confusion, Kade took off running, zigging and zagging through back alleys and abandoned buildings. He had no idea where he was going or what his plan was, all he knew was he needed to keep moving.

Chapter Twenty-Eight

Kade's lungs burned and he was out of breath. He was sucking back his oxygen supply at an unsustainable rate, depleting his only canister. Once it ran out, that was it, he would be dead. His legs were moving as quickly as possible, despite his limp.

It was midday so there was plenty of light, however, much of the sun was blocked by the tall buildings. He made it six blocks without encountering any danger, but he was still far from home. Ducking in an out of buildings, he navigated blindly through the dead city, heading down back alleys and back roads, trying to maintain a low profile. The city was massive, but with that, there were a lot of hiding spots for scavs as well, which made him nervous.

In the distance, he spotted movement so he ducked into a blown out wall and withdrew into the shadows. He lay in wait for a moment to catch his breath and to avoid being spotted. Blood soaked into his boot. He lifted up his pantleg to reveal a wound that didn't know he had. He would definitely need treatment at some point soon, but that wasn't likely to happen. Within seconds, a group of scavs ran past with their guns drawn. Kade retreated back against the wall and remained still.

When the timing felt right, Kade poked his head out of the building. Struggling to his feet, he steadied himself on his wounded leg and hobbled forward. He picked up his pace with each laboured step and made it another two blocks before stopping once again. To his delight, he began to recognize some of the buildings. He had been there before.

In his excitement, he threw caution to the wind and became careless. As he made his way down the middle of the street, he was spotted.

"Hey!" someone called out. "There he is!"

A shot rang out and Kade ducked his head. He could hear the bullet whiz by. There was another shot, then another. Parts of the ground exploded mere inches away from his fast-moving feet. He found refuge in one of the buildings. Bullets ricocheted off the brick and echoed throughout the street. Through deep inhalations, he kept the oxygen flowing through his body. The ever-depleting levels was constant on his mind. If he were to make it back to Endocrine, he would definitely need to re-up.

The scavs pursued on foot, but had stopped firing. Kade was in no condition to be involved in a foot chase, but knew the consequences of getting caught. Gritting through the pain, he kept moving, darting in and out of buildings in a sporadic and evasive pattern.

Breathing heavily, he needed to regain control over his heart rate not only to conserve oxygen and energy, but he felt like he was about to pass out at any moment. Evidently, he was no longer in the kind of shape he used to be where he could run for several kilometres in the scorching desert heat. Finding a spot in a building, he hunkered down in a dark corner.

Again, Kade thought about how much oxygen he was expending. It was like being invested in a stock with one's entire life savings, and then watching helplessly as the stock plummeted.

Crouching low with his back against a wall, Kade sat up and peaked out a small window. He could see several scavs. It appeared as though they had split up to look for him. Kade sized up one of the guys who was by himself, and felt as though he would be an easy target.

Looking around him, Kade found a sizable chunk of brick that was heavy, but could be held in one hand. He picked it up and then let out a deep breath to calm his nerves. Using the wall for assistance, he stood up and sneaked up on the lone scav.

The ground was made of loose dirt, which absorbed his weight and allowed him to move quietly, even as he was running. Plus, since everyone wore helmets, this acted as a barrier to dampen the sound.

Kade moved quickly almost as if he had forgotten about his injury. He covered the distance between him and the unsuspecting scav within seconds. When he was within arm's reach, Kade raised the brick high and clobbered the scav on the back of the neck. The scav went down, plowing face first into the ground. A plume of ash billowed out around him. Kade dove on top of him and began to club him repeatedly, bashing in the scav's chest with the rock.

With his heart rate elevated, Kade quickly searched the scav for anything of use — a weapon, disguise, oxygen canister. The only oxygen canister was the one in his helmet. Kade took a deep breath before removing his oxygen canister and swapping it out for the scav's canister. The scav's oxygen canister had significantly more oxygen than he had, which he was pleased about. It would buy Kade some more time. He could have kept both, but in doing so would bring about an agonizing and cruel death for someone who was likely just misguided or coerced into his depraved ways. That was in Kade's nature.

While crouching low, Kade ran across the street and hid once again. He needed to calm his nerves. His hands were shaking and he was breathing way too hard. He closed his eyes and attempted to regain control over his breathing. He recalled his time with the monks and how they taught him how to breathe and calm his mind and body. Like a Zen master, Kade took a moment to meditate. Despite being in the midst of a chaotic manhunt, Kade was in a state of relaxation in his mind and body. When he opened his eyes again, he had recalibrated. He wasn't so panicky and high-strung as he was before.

He slowly stood up and made his way through the building he was in. Traversing down hallways, through debris fields, and over piles of rubble, Kade emerged on the other side of the block. Through sheer luck had found his bike. He wasn't sure what sort of damage it has sustained in the crash, but it was his only means of escape.

Chapter Twenty-Nine

With a laser-intense focus, Kade hobbled toward his bike.

"Hold it right there!" a voice shouted.

Kade turned and saw a scav aiming a gun at him.

Raising his hands to show that he was unarmed, Kade said, "Your leader is dead."

"Shut up!"

"I didn't kill him. It was the women. They stabbed him a few blocks away."

"I said shut up. Get on the ground, now!" the scav commanded.

"It's okay, you're free," Kade said. "You no longer have to live in fear."

As the scav processed what Kade had told him, he lost a sliver of focus. Kade took advantage of this moment and

lunged forward, grabbing the barrel of the gun. A shot was
fired, but was diverted away. As the struggle ensued,
another shot rang out. Again, it narrowly missed. It was as if
they were dancing.

Kade threw all his weight into a punch that knocked the
scav's helmet clean off. Kade then rip the gun out of the
scav's hand. The scav was now on the ground, his head was
rattled, and he was desperately searching for his helmet,
which Kade was now standing over. Kade now had the gun
and all the power. He aimed it at the scav, but didn't have
the heart to pull the trigger. A young face stared up at him in
desperation. The scav was just a kid, no more than
seventeen. He was holding his breath, pleading with his eyes
for Kade to show mercy.

The last breath of the boy was held in his puffed cheeks.
Each passing second invoked even more panic as his body
absorbed the oxygen. Instead of shooting the boy, Kade
kicked his helmet in one direction while running in the
opposite. With his last bit of energy, the boy quickly
scrambled toward the helmet and shoved it back on his
head.

By now, Kade had a sizable gap between him and the
scav, and he was now armed. He tucked his arm and head
through the strap of the gun, which now hung by his waist,
and was making his way toward his bike. Just then, he felt
something press against his shin and immediately stopped
dead in his tracks. He had inadvertently tripped a wire.

Before he had time to react, a series of mechanisms were set in motion. Buried beneath the soot was a metal wire that sprang up like a cobra, wrapped around his leg and took his feet from underneath of him. In one fluid motion, Kade was swept off his feet and hauled high in the air. The force whipped him up so fast that it ripped his loose-fitted helmet right off his face. Kade was completely caught off guard, but had the wherewithal to take a deep breath.

Kade dangled upside down by both legs by a steel cable that stretched from one end of the street to the other. He felt like a fly trapped in a spider web. His arms, hair, and clothes stretched toward the ground. His view, now upside down, he saw the young scav approach. He looked down and saw the gun, which was now laying on the ground ten feet beneath him.

While still holding his breath, Kade reached for his knife, fumbled with it, but then gripped it firmly. With an aggressive sawing motion, Kade desperately tried to cut himself free, but it was no use. His knife was no match for the steel cable.

While he could hold his breath for a little over two minutes, he was already starting to slip. He estimated he had another thirty seconds or so before the last ounce of air burst from his lungs as he would instinctively inhale the toxic air.

Blood rushed to Kade's head, making him feel like he was going to pass out at any moment. His face turned a shade of purple and thick veins protruded from his face and neck. With his eyes barely open, he saw the boy standing underneath him. They made eye contact, but no words were spoken. Kade desperately wanted to beg the boy to spare his life, but he couldn't open his mouth.

That was it, he was down to his final ten seconds of life on Earth. A valiant effort making it this far post-apocalypse, but ultimately a life that meant very little. He would die a nobody, without making any meaningful contribution or impact. The world would carry on without notice.

Kade came to terms with death once again and said a silent prayer to his mother. As the final seconds counted down, he suddenly fell to the ground, slamming into a thick pile of ash that helped break his fall. Standing over him was the boy. His arm was stretched out and he was holding Kade's helmet. It was an offering. Without hesitation, Kade slipped the helmet on and inhaled a deep, life-saving breath.

"Thank you," Kade said. "You saved my life."

"And you saved mine. I think that makes us even. Go on, get out of here."

Kade saw the bike and ran to it before more scavs showed up. He struggled to lift it up, but eventually mounted it. He looked back at the scav, who was standing twenty-feet away, wearing his helmet. Kade gave him a nod as if to thank him once again. Without wasting a second thought, Kade accelerated so fast that the rear tire dug into the loose dirt until it found traction. A plume of dust shot up as Kade tucked his head and raced away.

Like a man with a new lease on life, he decided to escape while he still could. Given the circumstance, locating and retrieving the package was far too risky. Like a stealth panther, Kade made it through the city undetected. Once he reached the city limits, he looked back to see if he was being followed. He was not.

Chapter Thirty

Kade didn't suspect he was being followed, but still wanted to get as far away from the abandoned city as possible. Monitoring his oxygen intake, he was mindful of the time. He needed to make his oxygen last until he reached Endocrine. The display on his helmet told him that he had less than a day's worth of oxygen. With Endocrine less than a day away, it would be cutting it close. He could not afford any major detours or setbacks at this point.

A dull, nagging headache lingered, but he did his best to ignore it. What he couldn't ignore was the pain in his leg. As he pressed on, he stretched it out, which only seemed to make it worse. Just as he was thinking about stopping for a quick stretch and bathroom break, he caught movement coming from behind.

Heavy on the throttle, Kade continued to look over his shoulder, blasting through the hazy fog that had crept in. Riding high, he jockeyed the bike as it skipped across the uneven terrain. Navigating the sand dunes were exhausting and required a lot of strength and endurance to control the bike as it bounced around the rolling mounds. Without his drone and special helmet, it was also difficult to read the topography. To his eye, everything appeared to be flat and of the same colour.

Approaching a sand dune at high speed, Kade launched off it like a ramp, becoming momentarily airborne before slamming down, compressing the suspension to the max. Kade gritted in pain as his wounded leg begin to shake from the lactic acid that had built up.

The choppy and unpredictable landscape was taking its toll on him and his bike. It also made peering over his shoulder incredibly difficult and dangerous. When he hit a smooth patch, Kade snuck another glance over his shoulder. Racing toward him were large battle drones that were nearly impossible to escape, especially with the old bike he was riding.

The high-speed drones were closing the distance and were now within firing range.

Pff, pff, pff, pff – their guns started firing. Kade swerved back and forth to be as evasive as possible, but he knew he couldn't maintain these manoeuvres the whole way. It was only a matter of time before the drones had completely caught up to him. Once their sensors were close enough to lock onto him, he would be picked off with ease.

Turning his head for a brief moment, he only saw two drones. By the time he turned around, his front tire was already lifting off the ground. The bike launched off a sand drift, but this time he was unprepared. He lost his balance and was bucked off, slamming into the soft sand and he rolling to a stop.

Wincing in pain, he wasn't sure if anything was broken, but he didn't have time to worry about that at the moment. He lifted his head just in time to see his bike explode into a million pieces. The drones slowed to a stop and circled the perimeter, looking for Kade. Using his last bit of strength, he placed one forearm in front of the other and crawled behind a large dune.

He rolled onto his back and stared up at the sky. He was utterly defenseless. His only option was to bury himself in the sand. The drones continued to search the area. With their guns drawn and ready to lock onto a target, the high speed drones covered a 25 metre radius, scanning every rock, mound, and piece of debris. But they couldn't find Kade anywhere.

Satisfied that they had completed their mission, they retreated, disappearing into the fog in which they had come. Kade could hear the dissipating sounds, but remained buried for a few extra minutes just in case.

Feeling reasonably confident that he was in the clear, he emerged from the sand and dusted himself off. It was a close call, but he was definitely not out of danger just yet.

Hobbling to his feet, he made his way to what was left of his bike, some of the larger pieces were still in flames. There was absolutely nothing to salvage.

With only two choices — stay and die, or continue the rest of the way on foot, he started walking. Even though it was futile, he would rather die a fighter than a quitter. His injury, dehydration, and heatstroke didn't help matters, but those were the least of his concerns. His oxygen supply would surely run out before he reached any sort of civilization.

Chapter Thirty-One

Drenched in sweat, Kade's shuffling feet barely left the ground. His heavy eyes fought to stay open as his bone-dry mouth hung agape. With every ounce of strength and will, he continued putting one foot in front of the other. He knew it was a fool's errand since his oxygen supply would run out within the next ten minutes, and he was at least a day's walk away from reaching civilization, yet he persisted.

Depleted, Kade eventually collapsed face first into the sand. His last moments on this insufferable planet were near. As the last gasps of oxygen entered his lungs, alarms and buzzers began going off. He slapped the side of his helmet to silence the sounds. With his eyes closed, he baked under the hot desert sun.

In his final moments of despair, a glimmer of hope emerged in the distance. A traveller. Perhaps a mirage. He wondered if his mind was playing tricks on him. A black spec barreled toward him, growing larger by the second until he could almost reach out and touch it. He stretched his arm out and held it for a second before it too collapsed in the sand.

His brain was experiencing hypoxia — delusions brought on from a lack of oxygen. He would be dead within the minute.

A tire pulled up, the thick thread stopping mere inches from his face. A boot planted on ground, then another. Hands placed on his shoulder, rolled him over. A figure stood over him, blocking out the sun. A fresh oxygen canister placed in his helmet. Shallow breaths kept him alive. Then a voice entered his helmet. Delirium? He wondered if this was what death feels like? He could feel his consciousness slipping away. Too tired to move. Too exhausted to care. He was ready to be released from this harsh world.

"Kade?" the voice said. "Kade!" It grew louder. "Can you hear me? Kade, wake up!"

A tube was connected to his helmet. "Drink!" the voice said with urgency. A flicker of light kept him alive — a spark in his soul telling him to hang on and fight for a moment longer. He sucked back the cold liquid and could feel it all the way down.

"Hang on, Kade," the voice said again, this time it entered his brain with a little more coherence.

Kade's near lifeless body was becoming more lucid. Just then, he felt a small prick in his leg. An injection of some kind. Like a dimmer switch being turned on, he slowly began to regain a foothold on reality. His eyes opened, and his field of vision narrowed. Cali. What is she doing here? Is this really happening? He tried to speak, but only slurs came out at first. His frustration grew as he fought the biological constraints that bound him. "Ca...li," he mumbled softly.

"Kade!" Cali said. "I'm here. I'm here to save you. Don't worry, I won't let you die."

"You... left me."

"I'm here now."

There was an inaudible moan.

"Come, on, let's get you home."

Kade was assisted to his feet and then helped climb onto the back of his bike — the bike in which Cali had taken from him.

"My bike," he said.

"Was your bike. I stole it, remember?" Cali said, mounting the large bike.

"Why did you leave me?" Kade said.

"You really want to do this now?"

"Later may not come for me."

"Fine. I did what was best for both of us. I trust the monks took care of you well — fed you, provided you with shelter, got you off drugs, centered your being... or whatever. They did the same for me. I knew you were in good hands."

"What about you? Where did you go?"

"To take care of some unfinished business. Look, I'd love to catch up with you, but we don't have much time. We need to leave now. Can you hold on?"

"Yeah."

"Then let's get you home."

Cali accelerated, causing Kade to grip tighter around her waist. The back tire sunk into the ground and within seconds they were speeding toward Endocrine. Kade could hardly believe it.

"Ironic, right?" she said, communicating through their helmets.

"What's that?"

"When you found me, I was stranded in a desert with nothing. Then through serendipitous events, I ended up saving you in the same desert, but this time you were stranded with nothing."

"Some would call that fate," Kade said.

"Just goes to show you, it pays to be kind. You're welcome."

"Was that a compliment for me, or you?"

"Both."

Chapter Thirty-Two

Kade and Cali entered Endocrine a little past midnight, exhausted, broken, but alive. Many years ago, Cali had a place in Endocrine, she wondered if her things were still there. Together they drove to her apartment, which was not far from where Kade lived.

"I need to see if my mother is okay," Kade insisted.

"Now?"

"I'm not sure if she's alive."

"Either she's alive, but asleep, or she's dead and... well, also asleep. My point is, you can't show up in the middle of the night unannounced, smelling like a desert rat and looking like, well, a desert rat. Sorry, I'm tired — my brain is not too sharp right now to think of clever names to call you. Let's get you cleaned up and rested, then we can go over there. You said she hasn't seen you in months, right?"

"Yeah."

"Then what's a few more hours?"

As much as Kade didn't like to admit it, Cali had a point. They entered the apartment and stumbled through the door. The apartment was small and barely had any furniture. It looked like the kind of place that she could walk away from in five minutes and not leave anything behind. Cali went to her stash spot and found a dusty canister that had been untouched all the years she had been gone.

"I cannot believe this is still here," she said, plugging the canister into the filtration system. "It's like I never left."

"These units are air sealed, so it's like being in a vacuum. It sort of preserves everything."

Once in the door, Kade immediately peeled off his dirty and disgusting clothes and dropped them in a pile by the floor. They were covered in stains and smelled like they had been in a sewer. A crusted blood stain ran along the side of his right leg and he was afraid to look. The blood had clotted, but it was mashed with dirt and sand.

"Do you have a first-aid kit?" Kade asked.

"I'm not sure, I had some stuff in the bathroom at one point, but I haven't been here in years."

Cali returned with some clean clothes and told kade to wear them. "I found a first-aid kit," she said. "I'll get a bowl of warm water, and some rags."

Cali went to the kitchen, opened up some cupboards and drawers, and then returned with some rags.

"Are those clean?" Kade asked.

"Clean-ish."

Cali knelt down and tended to Kade's leg. "This is nasty," she said.

"I appreciate everything you've done for me."

"Don't mention it."

They took turns getting cleaned up. Cali went into the bathroom of her tiny apartment while Kade looked in the pantry for anything he could eat. She didn't have much, but he gorged on some stale crackers and a can of corn. Once Cali was done with the shower, it was Kade's turn. Once they were both clean, they sat in the living room.

"So what's the plan?" Cali asked, sitting on the couch.

"The good news is that no one knows that we know each other," Kade said. "That gives us an advantage. You can go to Mr. Saigon. Tell him you're a rider looking for work. See if you can gain intel."

"I think we should go together," Cali said. "I don't know this guy or what he's capable of."

"Fine. We'll go together. But first, I need to see if my mother is okay."

Later that night, Kade passed out on the couch while Cali slept on a single mattress less than ten feet away.

In the morning, Kade awoke feeling better, but still not one hundred percent. He had no idea what was wrong with him, but chalked it up to being physically and mentally exhausted over the past couple months. After a morning meditation and stretch, he and Cali left her apartment.

They walked down the street, their statuses set to unavailable, which hid their profiles from the network and allowed them to blend in discreetly without fear of being recognized by any of Saigon's goons.

They approached the apartment where Kade's mother lived, remaining hopeful that she would be inside. With a pit in his stomach, Kade entered the building and rode the elevator to the eleventh floor. Ms. Casey's apartment was at the far end.

Being separated by so much distance over the past few months, all he wanted was to be with his mother, to see her face again, tell her that he loved her and that he was sorry. Now, only a few paces separated him from his mother's door. He walked up with trepidation and took a deep breath to calm his nerves.

He placed his wrist against the sensor and scanned in. The door clicked open. He and Cali entered the apartment. It was dark and cold, showing no signs of anyone living there. His heart grew heavier with every step.

Kade entered each of the rooms anyway as Cali hung
back. She wasn't exactly the supportive type, but knew how
much Kade's mother meant to him.

"Did she move?" she asked.

Kade looked at her and shook his head. She couldn't see
his face, but could tell by the way he was hanging his head
that he was hurting inside. She stepped into him and
wrapped her arms around him.

"I'm sorry, Kade," she said.

Kade felt like someone had shoved a dagger through his
heart. He pulled away from Cali and needed a moment to
himself to collect his thoughts. He walked over and sat on
the couch. His posture deflated, slouching forward he rested
his head in the palms of his hands and cried.

"We all go sometime," Cali said. "On to a better place."

The words were meant to comfort him, but they missed
their mark.

"Let's go," Kade said.

Chapter Thirty-Three

The neighbourhood in which they lived was in a deteriorating state of disrepair. Rusted and hollowed out cars propped up on blocks — stripped of anything of value — littered the streets. Disenfranchised people walked sluggishly like high-tech zombies. Caged windows, graffiti, and trash were the de facto decor.

Being back in Endorcrine was surreal for both Kade and Cali. As for Kade, he was constantly looking over his shoulder, fearful of being followed. Ideally, he would lay low for a few days and recover, but he needed to learn about what had happened in his absence, and if his friend Tanjoban had suffered the same fate as his mother.

"As riders, we are sometimes hard to get a hold of," Kade explained as they walked through the seedy neighbourhood. "If we cannot find Tanjoban, it could just mean that he is out doing a delivery."

They first checked Tanjoban's apartment, but he was not there. Next, they looked around some of his favourite spots in his neighbourhood. The word on the street was he was no longer making deliveries as none of his regular clients had heard from him or seen him in months. This was troubling news. It would be absolute heartbreaking for Kade to have lost the only two people he cared about.

The last place Kade and Cali looked was Chu's Wisely Coffee Shop. A part of Kade was apprehensive to enter because he was now indebted to Mr. Chu. He was afraid it would be a debt he could not pay back. He wasn't exactly sure how Mr. Chu would respond to seeing him again, but figured upon telling his story and what he had been through, Mr. Chu would be sympathetic to his situation.

Cali and Kade entered the small coffee shop and looked around. They were tracked and monitored the moment they scanned in. It wasn't particularly busy so they were able to find a preferable seat near the back. Looking over the digital menu, which was a part of the surface of the table, they selected some items and placed their order. A timer counted down upon receiving payment, which permitted them to stay in the shop. In addition to the coffee and donuts, they were also billed for the amount of oxygen they would use over the next hour.

A moment later, Mr. Chu emerged from the back.

"Kade Casey," he said in a tone that didn't connote any hostility.

Kade removed his helmet and looked at Mr. Chu. "I bet you didn't expect to ever see me again," he said.

"I'm glad you're alive and well."

"I'm alive," Kade said.

Within seconds, their order was ready and delivered through an internal network of conveyor belts. A tiny door on the wall next to their table slid open and allowed them to grab their beverages and snacks.

"I presume you're not just here for the coffee and donuts," Mr. Chu asked.

"Your instincts are as sharp as ever," Kade replied.

"Take your time. When you're ready, come on back and we can have a chat. I'm sure you have a doozy of a story and I can't wait to hear it."

Cali followed Kade into the back where they met Mr. Chu. They all took seats around the desk in his office.

"This is Cali," Kade said. "She literally saved my life."

"Twice."

"She also left me for dead. Twice."

"It's nice to meet you, Cali. I'm excited to hear your story," Mr. Chu said, leaning back in his oversized chair with folded arms.

"Gosh, where shall I begin?" Kade said, searching his brain. "As you know, I got jumped by Saigon and his goons. I came to see you shortly after. Not only did they beat me within an inch of my life, but they took my entire stash and injected me with ghost. Looking back now, I think they did that to either keep me alive, or make me reckless so I would do the delivery, I'm not sure.

"After I came to see you and got my gear, thank you for that by the way, I left that night. I was still badly wounded, but the clock was ticking, so I rode for a few hours. I encountered my first set of troubles early into the trip when I got caught in a crazy sand storm. It nearly killed me, but luckily the bike you had procured for me ended up saving my life."

Kade continued to tell his story all the way up until arriving back into town the night before. The whole time, Mr. Chu looked at him with a look of astonishment that he somehow was able to survive.

"I'm truly sorry you had to endure this experience," Mr. Chu said, "but I'm sure this experience has made you stronger and wiser."

"Truthfully, I don't think there was any benefit that came from it," Kade said.

"I'm sure you may be overlooking some benefits," he said with a smile as he looked at Cali.

"I'm not sure about the wisdom part, but I definitely don't feel stronger. Right now, I feel drained."

"Are you off the drugs?"

"Yes, I'm clean."

"So you're back now, what are you going to do?" Mr. Chu asked.

"First of all, let me just say that I appreciate everything you've done for me and I have every intention of paying you back. I may need some time though. I need to see about my mother. I went by her place last night, but she wasn't there. It looks as though she hasn't been there in months and I am fearing the worst. Have you heard anything?"

"No, I have not, but I will ask around and keep my eyes and ears open."

"Thank you. I appreciate that. As for what I'm going to do... well, Saigon most likely wants me dead, my health is deteriorating, and I have nothing, not even a bike."

"What happened to your bike?"

"Cali stole it," Kade answered.

"I'm confused," Mr. Chu stated. "Cali is right here, why don't you just take it back?"

"Over my dead body," Cali said.

"As you can see, she's not the most cooperative person I've met."

"Interesting. Well, I can get you all new equipment," Mr. Chu offered. "I can help you get back on your feet and take care of whatever you need."

"You'd do that?" Kade asked.

"Of course," Mr. Chu said with a smile. "You need to pay me back, right? How are you going to do that without gear?"

"I really appreciate it," Kade responded graciously. "You won't regret this."

Chapter Thirty-Four

Lying low in Cali's apartment was the perfect spot to hide. Nobody knew Cali and more importantly, nobody knew she had any connection to Kade.

"Do you ever ask yourself, 'what's the point of it all'?" Kade asked.

"The point of what?" Cali responded.

"Life. Think about it, we live in this crazy world where the air is toxic, the waters are polluted, the people are shady, the leaders are corrupt. Ninety-five percent of the population, including animals, insects, and plants are dead. We struggle so hard in life and nothing ever comes easy. Family and friends are few, and any sort of optimism for the future seems dismal at best. There's no hope, no promise of a better tomorrow, no light at the end of the tunnel. I mean, at a certain point, as rational human beings, you have to question why we bother. Why continue on? For what purpose? What's the point of it all?"

"You're in a dark place right now, which is understandable, but I think it's clouding your judgement. Not everyone has this doom and gloom outlook as you. Sure, things aren't always rosy, but that has been true for many points throughout human history, but it always gets better. I think that's the hope that keeps people going. Hope that one day it could get better even if you can't see it now. If not for yourself, do it for your species. Make this place better for those coming after you."

"Did I ever show you this?" Kade asked, staring at a tiny object in the palm of his hand.

"What is that?"

"I'm not sure," Kade said. "The monks pulled it out of the back of my neck. I don't remember it being put in, but Kefu said the scar looked fresh."

"A tracking device perhaps?" Cali offered.

"Could be, but doesn't look like one. And it's not like Saigon is knocking at our door."

Just then, there was a knock on the door, which made them both stop talking and reach for their guns.

"Who the hell is that?" Kade asked.

"I'm not sure," Cali said, standing up slowly, approaching the door with caution. "No one knows we are here."

Kade stood at the end of a long corridor, gripping his gun tightly. Whoever were to come through the door would surely get blasted before taking their first step. Cali looked through the monitor, but didn't recognize the person on the other side. She looked at Kade and gave him a non-verbal cue to get ready.

Cali swung the door open and shoved a gun in the man's face.

"What do you want?" she barked.

"Whoa, don't shoot!" Tanjoban said, holding out his hands passively to show that he was unarmed.

"Tanjoban?" Kade said.

"Kade!"

Kade charged down the hall, colliding with his old friend, as they wrapped their arms around each other in a tight embrace.

"Kade, my brother," Tanjoban said. "It's so good to see you again, buddy. How the hell are you?"

"I've been better," Kade said.

"Tanjoban I presume," Cali asked. "I hate to interrupt this touching moment, but how the hell did you know we where here?"

"Kade texted me the address. I guess he forgot to tell you."

"I must have forgot I did that. My brain has been a little off these last couple of days."

"You should probably get that checked out. Did you hit your head?"

"Dozens of times. I've been beat up, shot at, dropped on my head from over ten feet, been in several accidents, some involving explosions... and those are just the ones I remember."

"I'm sure you just need rest. By the way, sorry I didn't text you back and just showed up out of the blue. I can't exactly check and reply to messages while I'm work. Besides, I thought it would be better to surprise you."

"I'm surprised," Kade said, showing the first signs of happiness all day.

"Yeah, me too. I nearly blew your head off. You shouldn't show up to someone's place unannounced."

Tanjoban joined Cali and Kade on the couch and together they caught up with each other's lives over the past three months. Like he had done with Cali and Mr. Chu, Kade launched into his story once again.

"What was it like staying at the monastery?" Tanjoban asked.

"Honestly," Kade paused. "I was in a really dark place, some would say I still am. I thought Cali had left me for dead, I was alone, and completely helpless. My body and mind were breaking down and I didn't know how much longer I had left, or how much more I could endure. Then I was saved. These monks brought me back to this amazing compound that they had reclaimed. They told me it was a former military base or something."

"That's so cool," Tanjoban said.

"They taught me a lot about centering myself and finding inner peace. I still have a long way to go before I achieve inner peace, but like NA, I take it one day at a time."

"So Cali, why did you leave him?" Tanjoban asked.

"I didn't leave him for dead if that's what you are implying. I like to think of it more as me bringing him to a place where I knew he would get the help he needed, which turned out to be exactly what happened. But truthfully... I was just looking after myself. I was desperate to escape the tyranny of the scav overlord who had enslaved me. Kade had a bike and I saw that as an opportunity, so I took it. We've talked about it since and made our peace with it."

"I learned more about Cali from the monks than from her," Kade added, coming to Cali's defense. "They told me that she had been there before and defended them against a bunch of scavs who were looking to kill them and take over their compound. She wouldn't let that happen. Underneath this rugged exterior, Cali has a heart of gold."

"Shut up," Cali said.

"Yeah, I was going to say, you two look good together," Tanjoban said.

Kade looked over at Cali with reverence in his eyes. In a world where hope was hard to come by, he was beginning to find a reason to live.

"So enough about me," Kade said, "What's been happening here?"

"A lot has changed," Tanjoban said. "I'm no longer a rider."

"Really? What happened?"

"I mean, I still take odd jobs, but that's not my main source of income."

"What do you do now?

"Actually, I got a job... with Saigon."

"Are you being serious? Doing what?"

"Security of all things."

"Security?"

"Yeah."

"What does that entail? Are you like his personal bodyguard or something?"

"No no, I'm just one of the guards in his building. I hardly ever see him."

"Wow," Kade said, unsure how to react.

"It's a job."

"Yeah, I hear you. Sometimes you gotta do what you gotta do. I've worked for him too so I can't really judge."

"The guy pretty much owns the city, so it's kind of hard to avoid working for him, ya know."

"May I ask what happened with my mother?" Kade asked sorrowfully. "I have not seen her, so I assume the worst."

"As a matter of fact, I do know what happened to your mother," Tanjoban said, pausing for effect. "Don't worry, she's fine."

"What! Are you being serious?" Kade said, leaping to his feet.

"Why do you think I took the job as Saigon's security? I relocated her. She's safe. I can bring you to her tomorrow."

"Does she know I'm alive?" Kade said, holding back tears.

"I don't know. I check in on her every couple of days and make sure she has everything she needs. I'm pretty sure that's not what Mr. Saigon had in mind when he told me to take care of her."

"Bro, I cannot thank you enough," Kade said, stepping forward and wrapping his arms around Tanjoban. "You are a true friend."

Kade could no longer hold back his tears as his emotions were in overdrive. Cali looked at the two and saw something in their friendship that she hadn't seen in a long time. It was a beautiful moment she got to be a part of and she felt something inside her change.

"Don't mention it. I'm just doing what any decent person would do."

"You're being modest and you know it. Seriously, I will repay you. Every last drop of oxygen, I swear."

The three continued to talk for hours, but Tanjoban had work in the morning and needed sleep. He hugged Kade and Cali and left close to midnight.

Now with Tanjoban gone, Cali and Kade were alone. There was clearly something on her mind, but Kade didn't ask her about it. Instead they stayed up and drank a bottle of wine, staring out at the city lights. They sat on the couch with all the lights off, basking in the dim glow from the city as it lit up the skyline and crept through the large windows.

"You know, when I was a younger," Kade reflected, "I used to think these lights were beautiful. The neon purples and blues, flickering across the sky. Holograms coming to life sixty stories tall, dancing on the sides of buildings.

Skyscrapers that literally touch the sky, disappearing in the clouds."

"Now how do you look at it?" Cali asked.

"I don't know," Kade said. "I guess I look at it more of what it represents. Having lived with the monks for a brief period of time, I've developed a new appreciation for life and what it means. There's more to living than bright lights and material possessions. It's about having meaningful relationships with people, sharing moments with them, and creating lasting memories."

In that moment, Kade looked over at Cali, locked eyes, and kissed her. Cali was caught off guard, but didn't pull back. She embraced the moment and allowed her heart to dictate her actions. She placed her glass of wine down and grabbed Kade's face, kissing him more passionately than he had kissed her. It was almost as if she was no longer in control of her actions. She had craved intimacy and physical touch for so long, it was almost reactionary. The two fell back on the couch, kissing aggressively and tearing off each other's clothes.

The moment was magical. Neither of them had experienced anything close to that level of romantic connection with someone. As they lay on the couch, caressing each other's sweaty bodies, Kade joked about how much oxygen they had just used.

"The universe works in mysterious ways," Cali said with an uncharacteristic smile. She was coming out of her shell, letting her guard down, and allowing Kade to see another side of her.

"Tell me about it," Kade said. "Who would have thought that a suicide mission would have led to us finding each other."

They shared a look and another kiss.

"I'm falling for you, Cali," Kade said, leaning over and kissing her on the forehead. "I know we just met not too long ago, but I can't imagine my life without you."

Cali didn't respond, almost as if she was putting her walls back up. Kade took notice. "I'm sorry... I—"

"No, it's not that. I have to tell you something, Kade," she said with a look of regret.

"What is it?"

"I... I'm not good at expressing my feelings, but let's just say that I like you, and I don't want to start off lying to you."

Kade was unsure what was coming next.

"You know when I found you in the desert?"

"Yeah."

"Well, I didn't come back to rescue you... I came back for the bounty."

"What?" Kade said, sitting up, allowing a blanket that covered them to slip off. Cali pulled it up to her neck and clutched it tightly.

"There's a bounty on your head. A big one. I went out to look for you since I know where I left you. I figured I might find you, take you back to the city, and collect a nice paycheque."

"When did you change your mind and decide not to turn me in? Wait, please tell me you've changed your mind."

"Yes, I promise," Cali declared emphatically, sitting up with him. "When I found you in the desert, all alone and helpless, that's when everything changed. I saw you as that little boy riding his bike, alone in the world. After hearing your story and knowing how much you must have suffered to get where you are... plus, the situation with your mother... that's when my heart melted for you. I decided to be your friend and really be there for you. In fact, you taught me that. You taught me that there's good people in the world, you taught me how to love. You gave me hope."

Cali started to cry, which Kade had never seen her do before.

"My name is Calista Gray, 24 years old, no family, no friends. All I have is you. This is me. I'm not perfect, but I strive to be better every day. I never thought I would say this to anyone, but... I'm falling for you."

Chapter Thirty-Five

Kade sat on his bike, adjusting his helmet. It felt good to be on a set of wheels again, back in his home city no less. He had waited a long time to see his mother and could not wait to lay eyes on her. For this, he went solo.

He pulled out of the underground parking facility and cruised through the city. It was midday, but it was dark and cold, consumed by perpetual state of dull orangey smog. People went about their day, most of them blissfully unaware of the evil underpinnings that controlled everything from an ivory tower. Compliance or ignorance, he was guilty of it too, but most were not living in fear as he was.

For some reason, he felt like an outsider who didn't belong. He felt more at home at the monastery. Returning to Endocrine felt like returning to a life that he had left behind.

Although his identity was cloaked, he knew there were ways around that. In the hyper-connected world in which he lived, it was next to impossible for a person to truly hide. The anxiety of not knowing what was coming was nearly crippling. At every stop, Kade was constantly looking over his shoulder, allowing paranoia to seep in and assume everyone was out to get him.

Following the address Tanjoban had given him, he maintained a low profile by choosing back roads that didn't have a lot of traffic. Upon arrival, he circled the block a few times just to ensure he wasn't being followed.

Pulling into an underground parking garage, he dismounted his bike and entered the building. According to Tanjoban, his mother was living on the fourth floor. His heart pounded with anticipation as he felt this day would never come.

He rode the elevator up and found his mother's unit. Now standing in front of the door, he scanned in, which captured his digital profile and sent an alert to the person on the other side. He could hear shuffling as he waited patiently in the hall. Some other people entered the hallway, which made him nervous. For a brief moment, he wondered if he had fallen into a trap. Keeping an eye on the others, he scanned in again.

The other people entered a suite on the same floor, which put his mind at ease. He was carrying a gun that he had acquired from Mr. Chu, but he didn't want to use it.

The door opened and Kade's mother immediately started to cry. It was as if she was looking at a ghost. She reached out, pulling her son inside, and hugging him.

"Kaden, my sweet little boy," she said, squeezing as hard as she could. "I'm so happy to see you."

The emotions where too overwhelming and soon Kade found himself sobbing uncontrollably as well.

"I love you, mama. You don't have to worry no more. Your baby boy is home."

Kade and his mother entered the living room of the small apartment and Kade saw how she was living. It was set up just the way she liked it, with food and oxygen to last her months.

"Tanjoban set all this up for you?" he asked.

"Yes, he's an angel. Please come inside, take off your helmet, I want to see your beautiful face."

"It's so incredible to see you, ma," Kade said, taking a seat on the couch and pulling his helmet off.

"You as well," she said, still teary eyed. "You have no idea how long I've waited to see your face again. To have you show up one day and sit with me, it's just... words cannot begin to explain. It's a dream come true."

"I feel the same way. Are you well?" Kade asked.

"These last couple of months for me have been really difficult — not knowing where you were, if you were alive and safe. I had to assume the worst and that broke my heart. I had to endure many stressful days and sleepless nights. A mother should never outlive her son and the thought of something happening to you absolutely crushed me."

"I felt your pain as well," Kade said. "I was beaten, drugged, and threatened. I was given an impossible mission and if I did not carry it out, they told me they'd kill you. I was given one week to deliver a package and after that week had passed and I was nowhere near the drop point, I feared the worst. Over the past three months, I have felt an incredible amount of guilt, crippling guilt, but I didn't give up. Well, actually, I did once. I tried to..." Kade stopped himself. "Let's just say I was in a very dark place. But I found a light that guided me. I made it back to you, so that's all that matters. I promise to put an end to all this and never leave your side again."

"That sounds nice. I'd like that."

"I found a girl," Kade said proudly. "I really want you to meet her. She saved my life, and she'll be the first to remind me that she did so on more than one occasion."

"I would love to meet her. What's her name?"

"Her name is Cali. She's... well, she's not like anyone I've ever met before. She's tough and doesn't take you-know-what from anyone. But she also has a kind heart.

Underneath, she's just as broken as the rest of us. I think we make a good team."

"That's so wonderful. I hope you two go on to raise a family and live happily ever after."

Kade laughed. "I don't know about all that, ma. It's still very early stages. We're not exactly official yet, but... I'm hopeful. For the first time in my life, I'm hopeful."

His mother smile adoringly and squeezed his hand.

"When did you get back?" his mother asked.

"Late last night, so I haven't fully recovered from my trip. I'm feeling a bit dehydrated."

"I'll fetch you some water," his mother said. "Would you like something to eat. I can make you some lunch."

"Lunch would be lovely, but please, allow me to make it for you."

"Don't be silly, you need to rest."

Kade proceeded to tell his mother how he went to her old apartment and asked around. "Nobody had heard or seen you in months. I didn't know where you were, what happened to you, or whether or not you were still alive. As soon as I found out from Tanjoban, I came to see you."

"So you didn't make the delivery?" his mother asked. "Did you ever find out what you were delivering? I can't imagine what would be so valuable that nearly got you killed?"

"Honestly, I have no idea what was in the package. I guess I will never know."

Chapter Thirty-Six

It was late at night when Kade decided to leave his mother's place. He remained positive and optimistic with her to not cause her any more worry, but there was something he wasn't telling her. His health was declining and he wasn't sure why. His body was breaking down. He was experiencing fatigue, lightheadness, slower reaction time, and spouts of vertigo. He figured it was the trace amounts of ghost still lingering in his body or he was concussed. He planned to see a doctor soon, but had some other things he needed to sort out first.

Through the visor of his helmet, Kade analyzed the neon holographic data that glowed in the display. The temperature was dropping, which gave him all the more reason to get home as soon as possible. As it was close to midnight, there were few vehicles on the road, most of which were automated and moved in very predictable patterns. This made speeding around them fun.

Riding through the city back to Cali's apartment, he pulled up to a stoplight and cranked up his oxygen in-take. The sudden rush of oxygen flooded his bloodstream and gave him the acuity and awareness he needed to get home safely.

To his left, a vehicle pulled up next to him. He looked over at the tinted windows and saw his reflection. Then the window rolled down and a gun barrel protruded.

"Pull over," the unidentified man demanded.

Without giving it a second thought, Kade immediately accelerated through the intersection, nearly being stuck by opposing traffic. His heartrate elevated and his adrenaline kicked in. The vehicle gave chase, but was quickly left in the dust as Kade took off like a bolt of lighting, swerving in and out of traffic. He was one of the world's top riders and while his reaction time was diminished, he was still able to outrun just about anyone.

As he made several evasive turns, he considered lying low, but knew that wasn't a good long-term strategy. He wasn't feeling well and wanted to get back to Cali as quickly as possible.

Streaks of light whizzed by as he maintained his speed, creating even more distance between him and his pursuer. As he focused on the road ahead, two other bikes emerged from adjacent streets and began to follow him. Unsure who they were, Kade kept a watchful eye on them through the rear display projected in his helmet visor.

The two other riders closed the gap and were now right on his tail. Being careful to watch both the road and the two riders, Kade had to process a lot of data at once. His vision would go through bouts of blurriness and lights became too bright causing him to see spots. He did his best to adjust.

The other riders pulled out their guns and started firing at him. The shots whizzed by his head and nearly took him out. He ducked and fired off a rapid burst of three shots of his own. The last bullet found its mark, hitting the front tire of one of the riders, causing him to flip end over end.

Kade kept moving. The second rider was still in pursuit, following him like a shadow through the city streets, which were illuminated by a neon glow from the city centre. Kade swung his arm behind him and watched carefully in the rear video, attempting to aim. The rider kept swerving and Kade was too afraid a stray bullet would hit an innocent bystander. That's when he remembered his drone. He had received a new one from Mr. Chu.

With a simple command, the drone blasted out of the back of his bike and rocketed toward the sky. Guided by Kade's voice, the drone came back down with the same velocity and slammed into the chest of the pursuing rider. The rider fell backward off his bike, slamming on the pavement and rolling to a stop.

Kade watched the whole thing in the rear video display. With traffic moving around them, he reduced his speed and circled back around. He pulled up next to the downed rider who was writhing on the ground clutching his chest. Kade dismounted his bike and approached with caution, still brandishing his weapon. In the distance, he could hear sirens closing in on them.

"Who sent you?" Kade demanded.

His arm stretched out and he took aim at the rider's head.

"Saigon," the man uttered.

"Why?"

"Bounty," the man said, coughing up blood. "There's a bounty on your head. Nearly everyone in the city is looking for you."

"How much is the bounty?"

"250,000 units," the man said. "100,000 if you're dead."

Kade quickly mounted his bike and took off. With this news, he had received the confirmation in which he feared — this was not something that Saigon had forgotten about. A bounty that high only meant one thing — whatever was in that package was even more valuable than he had previously thought.

Chapter Thirty-Seven

Kade arrived back at Cali's place with a distraught look on his face.

"Is everything okay?" she asked.

"Three men tried to kill me... or kidnap me, I'm not sure."

"Are you okay?" Cali said, rising to her feet.

"Yeah, I'm good. I managed to evade them, but one of the men, I took him out and approached him. I asked who sent him and he told me that there is a bounty on my head. Undoubtedly the same bounty you were once after."

"We knew this was a likely scenario," Cali said. "A bounty like that is going to attract nearly everyone in the city. It's only a matter of time before someone gets you."

"I can't live like that," Kade said, still pacing.

"Okay, so what do you want to do?" Cali asked.

"This has to end. We need to go see Saigon."

Cali and Kade exited together and rode to Mr. Saigon's massive empire. Kade wasn't sure what to expect when they arrived. They pulled up much like he had done a hundred times in the past and were let in by security. Upstairs, Saigon watched on the monitors. He wasn't expecting to ever see Kade again.

Standing in the impressive entryway, Cali hadn't seen anything like it. It looked like a luxurious hotel. Crystals and chrome, polished brass and rich woods — the place was an opulent display of modern architecture and aesthetics, mixed with traditional textures. She felt a sense of awe as she looked around. She had been so removed from modernity that she felt a little out of place. She also had experience with evil dictator types and didn't want to fall victim to any traps.

While passing through one of the security checkpoints, Cali grew more nervous.

Escorted by security, they entered the elevator and rode it to the top floor. The doors opened directly in Mr. Saigon's office. The large room seemed to extend endlessly in all directions. The floor to ceiling windows provided stunning views of Endocrine that few ever got to see.

"The prodigal son returns," Mr. Saigon said with a sinister smile.

The towering man with an impeccably pristine three-piece suit sat on a throne-like chair behind a beautiful rose wood desk. Kade didn't say anything, he was holding back. He was so enraged at the sight of Mr. Saigon and wanted to charge at him and rip his eyes out of his head.

"And who might you be?" Saigon said in a somewhat flirtatious tone, turning his attention toward Cali.

"You can call me Cali — the bounty hunter that brought you Kade Casey — alive."

Kade turned toward her in shock, but before he could say anything, Cali had jammed a taser in his ribs, flipped a switch, which sent a thousand volts of electricity through his body, not enough to kill him, but enough to incapacitate him. Kade's muscles spasmed uncontrollably as he collapsed to the floor and continued to convulse.

Cali stepped over him and demanded payment. "I believe the offer was two-hundred and fifty thousand units."

Mr. Saigon didn't look pleased, but played along as if he had every intention of paying the bounty. "Of course," he said. "Right this way."

Cali followed closely behind.

Mr. Saigon walked over to Kade, knelt down, and held a device to the back of his neck. Without saying a word, his face said it all. He stood up with a look equivalent to a calm before the storm and asked sternly, "Where's the implant?"

"The what?" Cali asked.

"One of you has it," Mr. Saigon said, stepping over Kade and walking right up to Cali. His towering figure and deep authoritative voice was enough to intimidate anyone, but Cali wasn't backing down.

"Look, I have no idea what you're talking about," Cali said defensively. "You asked for Kade Casey, I delivered you Kade Casey. I'm not leaving without my payment."

Mr. Saigon paused for a moment, almost as if he were attempting to read her thoughts. He reached out with the quickness of a jungle cat and snatched Cali by the neck and lifted her in the air. She looked like a small child compared to Mr. Saigon.

Cali shoved the taser into Mr. Saigon's armpit and squeezed the trigger expecting him to release her. But instead, he just flashed his devilish grin and threw her across the room like a ragdoll. Her body smashed into a table and knocked it over.

Kade was still on the ground, unresponsive, and not moving. Tanjoban was also in the room. He froze in the moment unsure when to reveal himself. He remained on guard, waiting for the perfect moment to strike.

Mr. Saigon became completely enraged. He first kicked Kade in the stomach and charged over to Cali like a bull. "Where is it?" he shouted as spit flew out of his mouth. By now, Cali had returned to her feet and realized she was outmatched. With no time to think and nowhere to run, Cali was cornered. Mr. Saigon grabbed a hold of her again. With the strength of a silverback gorilla, he pinned her up against a wall and began to squeeze her windpipe closed. Cali's face was starting to turn purple and a look of panic came over her. Her eyes looked over at Tanjoban, which prompted him to jump into action.

Just then, a loud gunshot rang out, echoing throughout the office. Shattered glass, the sound of whistling air escaping the room, the bustle of a busy metropolis many stories below. Tanjoban stood with his gun steadied, now taking aim at Mr. Saigon.

"Let her go," he commanded.

Mr. Saigon complied and Cali collapsed to the floor, gasping for breath. He turned to look at the broken window, which was no longer acting as a barrier to the toxic outside atmosphere.

Tanjoban locked his eyes on Mr. Saigon while taking the necessary steps forward to his fallen friend. He crouched down and checked on Kade. He had a pulse, but it was faint. "Cali, get over here," Tanjoban said with urgency, still keeping Mr. Saigon at bay.

"You're a dead man," Mr. Saigon said with an expressionless face. "All of you are dead." His expression changed ever so slightly from melancholy to pleasure as if he was fantasizing about killing them.

Chapter Thirty-Eight

Cali and Tanjoban helped Kade to his feet, but he was still very much out of it. "Keep him alive," Mr. Saigon said. I want to have the pleasure of killing him.

Tanjoban had heard enough. He went into a complete rage and shot Mr. Saigon several times until him emptied the clip. Mr. Saigon fell backward over his desk and out of sight.

Tanjoban ran up to a locked cabinet and raided it for all the canisters. There were over 100, but it was more than he could carry.

"Come on, let's go!" Cali said.

Tanjoban loaded them all in a bag and then the three made a fast exit.

"Hang in there, buddy," Tanjoban said. "We're going to get you out of here."

The elevator barely made it down three stories before it stopped abruptly. An alarm was sounded, which sent the team into a panic. Kade was on the floor of the elevator, pale, and barely conscious.

"What's wrong with him?" Cali asked, crouching to her knees.

"I'm not sure. How much voltage did you use?"

"I barely touched him," she said. "That was the plan."

"What's-his-face kicked him pretty hard, maybe he's suffering from internal bleeding or something."

"Kade, wake up," Cali said, slapping him gently on his face. His eyes opened a crack. "Listen to me, we have to get out of here. Are you able to walk?"

"You guys go," Kade said softly.

"We're not leaving you here. You'll die."

"I'm already dying."

"That's why we need to get you out of here."

"No, you don't understand," Kade said. "I'm sick. I've been sick for a while. I won't make it. Just go."

Cali looked at Tanjoban who was out of answers and growing anxiously impatient by the second. "Come on,

Kade," Cali said with glossing eyes. "You have to get up. There's still time."

"This is the end for me," his said with a whisper. "But a new beginning for you."

"Cali, we have to make a decision now," Tanjoban said. The alarm still blaring in the background adding even more urgency to the situation.

"This can't be the end," Cali said. Her face tightened up, her eyes squinted, and tears began flowing freely down her face and dripping onto Kade. She leaned in and threw her body on top of Kade. She held him, sobbing uncontrollably. It was a rare emotion for her as she had been so bottled up for so many years. She hadn't allowed herself to get close to anyone. Since Kade came into her life, he had taught her how to love again. Seeing him like this was a real gut-punch for her.

She could almost feel Kade's life slip away in her arms, that's when she clamped on tighter. Tanjoban was just as distraught, but knew his moment of grieving would need to come later. He reached down grabbed Cali by the shoulder and pulled her off. She stood up and looked down at Kade, who was motionless on the cold and sterile elevator door. his eyes were closed and he no longer appeared to be breathing.

"We can't just leave him," Cali said through irrational thoughts of desperation.

"We must," Tanjoban said. "Unless you would like to join him."

Chapter Thirty-Nine

"You think he's dead?" Tanjoban asked, staring blankly out the window of Cali's apartment.

"I felt him slip away in my arms."

"I meant Saigon."

"How can you think of Saigon right now?"

"Because if he's not dead, then we are. I shot the man like ten or eleven times."

"Sounds like he'd be dead to me," Cali said.

"You never know with Saigon. He fell behind his desk. Until I see him dead, I won't ever feel safe."

"So what next?" Cali asked.

"We have enough canisters to last us a few months. I suggest we lay low and wait for this dust to settle.

Cali looked down at the rice-sized implant that was pulled out of the back of Kade's neck "What is this thing?" she said, flipping the tiny tube around in her hand.

"Whatever it is, it must be very valuable. Whatever package Kade was delivering must have been a decoy — he was the package."

"Do you know anyone you can trust with the knowledge, or technology, to analyze this thing?"

"I know a guy," Tanjoban said, retracting from the window and looking at Cali like a man with a plan. "What do you say we take that thing down to our friend Mr. Chu and see if he knows what it is?"

"Do you really think that's a good idea? I mean, suppose it is something powerful or dangerous, we won't want it to fall into the wrong hands."

"Good point. Let's stash it somewhere safe and where no one would ever think to look. Then we'll pretend we don't have it, but that Kade told us about it. See if Mr. Chu knows anything."

"I feel more comfortable with that plan," Cali said.

Cali and Tanjoban waited a few days before surfacing. During that time, they continued to grieve the loss of their friend. Tanjoban shared stories Kade, which only made Cali's heart grow fonder of him.

By the end of the week, Cali and Tanjoban had left the apartment and were now standing in front of Mr. Chu.

"I'm sorry for your loss," Mr. Chu said.

"Thank you," Tanjoban said.

Mr. Chu led them into the back where they could speak privately. Cali trailed behind, following Mr. Chu and Tanjoban into his office. She was constantly on guard, looking around anxiously, expecting to be walking into a trap.

They sat down in Mr. Chu's office and he asked them the reason for their visit.

"We were wondering if you heard about Mr. Saigon's death?"

Mr. Chu paused for a moment and looked at them. "I have heard rumours, but nothing concrete," Mr. Chu replied. "Perhaps you know more than me."

"Just the same rumours as you," Tanjoban said.

"Whenever you have a major player removed from the game, it creates a void. According to Game Theory, that void must be filled. One of two outcomes could happen. There could be a direct transfer of power — a successor if you will who takes over the throne and assumes that role. But we know Mr. Saigon did not have any children, and so far no one has come forward as a successor."

"What's the second scenario?" Tanjoban asked.

"The second scenario is a power struggle between competing forces. The power will shift partially or fully to whoever has the means and desire to acquire it. I suspect the latter. In the coming months, we may expect a new leader to rise and take over the city."

"Yourself perhaps?" Tanjoban asked.

Mr. Chu chuckled. "I'm an old man, and I enjoy my life as it is."

"I feel like this is the calm before the storm," Cali said.

"Whatever happens, it cannot be worse than what we have seen in our lifetimes. We are all strong people. We will find a way to survive," Mr. Chu replied.

"We always do."

"Was there something else you wanted to ask me?" Mr. Chu asked.

Tanjoban looked and Cali, then back and Mr. Chu. He leaned in and said, "You know, something just isn't sitting right with me about this whole mission," he said. "Mr. Saigon paid Kade ten canisters to deliver a package, right?

"As you know, that is a very generous offer — ten times the typical amount of any offer I have even heard of for a delivery. Now, granted it was a suicide mission and Saigon had no intention of ever fulfilling that payment, but here's where it gets interesting. The bounty on Kade's head was more than ten times the initial offer. So whatever Kade was carrying must have been very valuable."

"Perhaps it was bogus offer and would boycott payment once he got what he wanted," Mr. Chu said. "Nevertheless, Kade, or whatever was in that package, was valuable to Saigon."

"We don't know what was in the package because it was never recovered, but if you ask me, I think Kade was the thing that was valuable."

"Oh," Mr. Chu said. "What makes you say that?"

"Upon Kade's return, he mentioned experiencing neck pain at some point in the journey. With the help of Cali, they removed a little implant of some sort from the back of his neck."

"We didn't know what it was," Cali added. "We figured it was some kind of tracking device so we destroyed it."

"What did this object look like exactly?" Mr. Chu asked.

"It was a small cylindrical object no bigger than a grain of rice. It was smooth, metallic, and had no markings that we could see with our eyes. There was no way to open it. It didn't make any noise. We had no idea what it was or how it got there, but perhaps this was what he was unknowingly transporting. The actual contents of the package may have been completely meaningless, a decoy."

Mr. Chu looked very puzzled indeed.

"Based on what you've heard, what do you think it was? And could it be connected to Saigon in any way?"

Mr. Chu took a moment before responding. "You said this tube was metallic?" he asked, directing his question to Cali.

"Yes. Due to its size, we didn't get a good look at it, but there must have been something inside. Some nanotech perhaps. Too small for the naked eye to examine and of course, we didn't have a microscope."

"Well, then, it could have been anything," Mr. Chu said. "However, to really analyze this conundrum, let's first take a step back. We shall not look for answers in the micro, but in the macro."

"Okay," Tanjoban said.

"In order to learn more about this item, we first must ask ourselves some basic questions about what we know, which are the origins of it. As we likely agree, it belonged to Mr. Saigon."

"Yes, I believe that to be true."

"Very well. So the next question we must ask is, what is the ultimate goal of a person in Saigon's position? A man

who seemingly has everything — money, power, fame...
What would a person living in this world want?" Mr. Chu
asked.

The question didn't elicit an immediate response so Mr.
Chu reiterated the question in another way. "If you were Mr.
Saigon, what would you want?"

Cali was the first to offer an answer. "Security."

"Why?" Mr. Chu shot back.

"I would want to protect what I have for as long as
possible. I would assume people would be constantly after
me, trying to take me out."

"Okay, good. What else?"

"I mean, if it were me," Tanjoban said. "And I assume me
and Saigon have different values and life goals. But, I would
try to make the world a better place."

Again, Mr. Chu was quick to ask a follow-up question.
"What does a better world look like to you?"

"Everyone's basic needs are met — environmental
stability, clean air, food, and shelter for everyone."

"Why is that important?"

"A world that is good for everyone is a world that is good
for me."

"So what I hear you both saying are versions of the same thing, which is that you want a good life for as long as possible?"

"Yes."

"So you two ultimately arrived at the same conclusion — security and prosperity."

"I guess so."

"Now, what are some ways a person could ensure their security and prosperity?"

"Weapons," Tanjoban said. "You could have an army protect you in an impenetrable fortress."

"Okay, what else?"

"Love?" Cali suggested.

"Interesting," Mr. Chu stated, leaning forward in his chair. "Can you elaborate?"

"As Machiavelli said, there are two ways to rule — fear and love. If the people love you, they won't come after you."

"As I'm sure you know, as much as you try, not everyone will love you, so pursuing love as a strategy wouldn't guarantee a person's security. And we also know that Saigon was not trying to get people to love him. What else? It can be completely outside of the box."

"Immortality," Cali suggested.

"Very good, Cali," Mr. Chu said. "So if a person is immortal, then that would be the ultimate form of security, right?"

Tanjoban and Cali both nodded.

"Let's chase this whimsy and see where it leads us, shall we? What are some ways a person can achieve immortality?"

"Is this a trick question?" Tanjoban asked.

"No, we're just brainstorming here," Mr. Chu replied.

"Superpowers, a magic genie, a miracle," Tanjoban suggested, unable to take the question seriously.

"Technology," Cali said. "In theory, there could be technology that could rejuvenate a person's cells so that they can live forever."

"Ok, good," Mr. Chu said with a smile. "So technology that a keeps a person alive. That would be very valuable. And we all know technology is really about information. Could it be that Kade was transporting information in a tiny drive embedded in his neck?"

"If Saigon had this technology, why have Kade need to deliver it to Tri-city?" Tanjoban asked. "Why not use it to keep yourself alive?"

"Perhaps Saigon is still alive?" Mr. Chu said, giving them all a moment of pause. "As for why he delivered it, perhaps it was for a trade of some kind, or the technology was not fully developed."

"Do we know who he was supposed to deliver this package to?" Cali asked.

Everyone looked around the room blankly.

"Then perhaps we've reached the end of the road with our deductive reasoning. To truly solve this mystery, we need more information."

"Any suggestions on how we could acquire more information?" Tanjoban asked.

"I know a guy you can speak with. Perhaps he can help you. But it requires some travel."

About the Author

Edward Mullen is a novelist, blogger, vlogger, and podcaster from Vancouver, Canada.

Born and raised in beautiful British Columbia, Edward developed a love for the wilderness. This love, combined with an innate curiosity about all things, eventually spawned a healthy imagination for storytelling.

Despite spending a lot of his time indoors writing, Edward continues to enjoy the outdoors. He is an avid tennis player, mountain biker, snowboarder, runner, and traveler.

For more information about Edward Mullen, such as his podcast, blog, vlog, or upcoming books, please visit:

www.EdwardMullen.com

Zero Introduction

Thank you for reading The Rider. If you're looking for another cyberpunk book to read, check out Zero. I've included the introduction and the first two chapters for you to preview. I've also made this book into an audio book if you are interested. It's available on Audible and YouTube.

***

Displaced workers, a robot uprising, billions of lives lost.

The Automation War was inevitable. An unstoppable force of hyper-connected, uninhibited, carelessly misinformed people, hurling toward the edge of a cliff. A runaway train of capitalism and greed with no one at the controls. The unrelenting momentum of progress created by our insatiable appetites for innovation. No one able to stop what so many could see coming. Our fates were sealed.

The year is 2080, World War III is a recent memory, and the scars still remain. Billions have died, systems have collapsed, and the planet is in a state of disrepair.

It's now five years after the war and the governments of the world have fallen into the hands of an anonymous group of rogue hackers who call themselves The Shadow. They control every aspect of society from the economy, healthcare, education, justice, and law enforcement. They've eradicated disease, hunger, and poverty, but most importantly, they maintain peace and order.

There are no more terrorists plotting against the collective, no mental health disorders, no wars, and no crime. The only people permitted to live on Earth are law-abiding, healthy, educated, and productive members of society.

Using embedded chips, they track everyone's productivity, health, social status, and even emotional state. Based on these metrics, individuals are given a rank based on their social utility. Each person who exists is a vital part of the whole, contributing some net utility to the species.

However, under the guise of a seemingly benevolent agenda, they have created a climate of fear. Their radical policies are met with a lot of controversy and resistance.

Those who dissent, disappear. Those who do not maintain the required level of net productivity, emotional well-being, and financial stability as determined by The Shadow, which includes many of the elderly, are removed. What that means exactly, no one really knows, and no one dares to question the almighty authority. They could be watching, listening, plotting against you.

You could be next.

Zero Chapter One

"I was being followed, it was obvious. To the untrained eye, you know, someone just going about their day, not paying attention to their surroundings, they probably wouldn't have even noticed. But I noticed. I notice everything. They stood out like sprinkles on icing — a man 'waiting' for a bus across the street with an unmarked van parked fifteen feet away; a Goliath-looking mouth-breather, dragging his knuckles and sipping coffee; another man on a park bench feeding the ducks... They think they're being subtle, but they're not. Sometimes our eyes connect and I give them a wink or a nod… my little way of saying, 'I see you.'

"At this point, I'm not sure who they are or what they want, but so far they've kept their distance. Never once interacting with me. This went on for several days.

"I can think of about a dozen reasons why someone would want to follow me. The worst case scenario would land me minor jail time, but more likely just probation and a fine. Good luck getting me to pay though, I spent all my money on… well, I'm not going to say her name. That's another story altogether. Point is, I wouldn't be surprised if I've popped up on a few watchlists due to my browser history, which I won't go into.

"As I was saying, my guess is that some covert government organization wants to ensure I'm not a terrorist. If that's true, then let them follow me, I have nothing to hide. In fact, sometimes I behave in a sketchy manner just to mess with them, you know what I mean?

"So anyway, I returned from lunch one day and meandered through a sea of cubicles until I arrived at my desk. I removed my jacket and took a seat at my desk. Nobody was really paying attention to me.

"Something just didn't sit right, you know? Thinking back, it could have been the fish tacos I had for lunch. Come to think of it, it did give me a little case of hot bum if you know what I mean, but, I digress.

"What I remember feeling at the time was this insurmountable, gut-wrenching paranoia. Now, to be fair, I tend to sway a bit heavy on the paranoid side, but this was extra. And as you can see, given my current situation, I had a right to be a little paranoid.

"But it was the build-up that really took its toll on me, you know? The days of constantly looking over my shoulder, sleepless nights, not knowing who or why I was being followed. The anxiety of that isn't a pleasant thing to deal with as I'm sure you are all aware. It was like psychological warfare, and I'll admit, it was really starting to get to me, you know? I felt as though I was beginning to break down mentally and lose grip of my sanity.

"So I'm at my desk and I posture up a bit so that my head was sticking up over the cubicle wall. I saw my manager looking at me and I wondered — is he looking at me because I'm looking at him, or does he know something I don't?

"Nothing ever came of that, I just thought I'd mention it to give the story a little more context. So I decided I was done for the day so I left my coat and backpack at my desk and snuck out the back. I did this from time to time, especially on Fridays, or when my manager wasn't in the office.

"I exited the building without being seen by any of my coworkers and headed home. I got a few blocks away from where I live, and I saw a man walking his dog, a jogger stretching on a stoop, a mail carrier delivering packages. All ordinary stuff, right? But something about it seemed off. I then spotted the same van from earlier and realized they're all around me. They've been following me and have me surrounded and I yet to know why, or even who these people are. As you can imagine, I'm more than a little freaked out. I should mention that they've never come to my neighbourhood before, I mean, as far as I know. I was nervous and sweating profusely, my heart was pounding with anticipation because I knew something was about to go down. You know that feeling? It's almost like time slows down or something, it's really weird. I picked up my pace and began walking faster than usual.

"I then decided right then and there to be bold. It was like this wave of courage came over me. I was like, you know what, I'm sick of not knowing what this is all about. I'm going to confront them.

"Just as I was approaching the dog walker and about to speak, I hear a voice say my name, 'Mr. Jacobs.' It was a deep voice, the stern kind that you'd hear as a kid and make you piss your pants in fear. Nevertheless, it was a voice that I didn't recognize. And I should point out that I never interact with any of my neighbours.

"I turn around and see a tall man with broad shoulders. Our eyes met, not in a romantic way, I don't want any of you getting the wrong idea about me. But I will say this, he was handsome. I'm not ashamed to say that. He had a full head of hair and brawny jawline, but looked as though he'd been in a few tussles if you know what I mean. Call it a rugged handsome if you will. His presence made me feel a little, I don't know… insecure about my masculinity.

"'Can we have a word with you?' the man said to me in an authoritative tone.

"'What about?' I replied. I then said, 'If this is about my search history, I can explain.'

"I soon realized this was not about my search history.

"'Please, come with us,' the man said.

"'Who are you?'" I demanded. 'Who do you work for? What is this about?' I had a million questions, none of which were answered.

"'We have some questions for you,' he said to me.

"Next thing I know, two men approached me from the rear.

"I'm not sure why I decided to run, I guess I was in a fight or flight moment and my brain just shut down and my instinct took over. Before I knew it, my legs were moving beneath me and I was running as fast as I could down the street. I was hoping my neighbours would see me and call the police, or intervene in some way, but I know now that was foolish thinking.

"So I'm running, right… my adrenaline kicked in and for a split second I think I'm an athlete and my cardio will carry me for days if need be. Well, I didn't even make it fifteen feet before my body went numb and I collapsed to the ground. My head bounced off the pavement and put me in a bit of a daze. That's why I have this cut on my forehead.

"I was a little out of it after hitting my head, but the next thing I remember was the men standing over me, dragging me to my feet, and then shoving me into their van. It all happened so quickly and I was still in a bit of a daze. At one point I even questioned if this was real or if I was dreaming. It was all very surreal, you know? Perhaps some of you had a similar experience.

"They didn't handcuff me or read me my rights, which I thought was weird."

"Man, would you please shut the hell up? You talk too damn much. I can't hear myself think," a voice said from the back of the bus.

"Nah, let the brother speak," another man said.

"It's okay, I was done," Dane said.

"Go on, continue your story," another random voice encouraged.

"I mean, there's nothing really more to tell," Dane said to the group of strangers packed on the bus with him. "The last thing I remember was being in the van and then waking up here. I don't know how long it has been, what they did to me, where we're all going. In fact, I don't really know who any of you people are other than what you've told me. For all I know, you could be working for them."

"We're all handcuffed on this damn bus together. What makes you think that you're so important that someone would go to all this trouble to try to trick you? And to what end? You just told us a long boring story about how the worst thing about you was having porn on your search history."

"It wasn't porn actually, I was searching weapons and how to make a—"

"Man, I don't give a damn what you do in your spare time. All I know is that we need to figure out why the hell we are all on this damn bus, who put us here, and where we're going."

"That's what we're trying to do," another voice spoke. "We should hear each other's stories. Maybe there'll be some common thread that'll tell us why we're all here."

"I agree," a lady from the middle of the bus said. "At the very least, it'll pass the time."

"What's up with your man back there?" someone asked, directing the question to a quiet man at the back of the bus. "What's your story, dude?"

Everyone turned toward the man who was in the very last row of the bus. He hadn't said a word to anyone. He didn't even look out the window. The entire ride, he just had his head down. Then all of a sudden, the bus slammed on its breaks, causing everyone to jolt forward in their seats.

The automated bus stopped abruptly in the middle of nowhere. Trees and mountains surrounded them and a barren highway stretched out for miles in both directions.

"What's happening?" one man asked.

"Why are we stopping here?"

For a few minutes, the entire busload of people began to feel uneasy about the situation. They were all bound by their hands and feet and were secured to their seats. Then, their electronic shackles suddenly released. Everyone looked around nervously and massaged their wrists. A few stood up while others remained in their seats and looked out the window.

Without saying a word, the man from the back of the bus wheeled out from his position and rolled down the aisle. Until that moment, no one had any idea that he was bound to a wheelchair. The other passengers couldn't help but stare, curious to find out what he was up to.

The man reached the front of the bus and just as he was about to exit, he turned to everyone and said calmly, "They'll be here soon. I advise everyone to escape now while you still can."

Zero Chapter Two

Confusion, fear, and uncertainty swirled throughout the bus as people stared at the paraplegic man who was seemingly staging an escape. Inaudible murmurs began until someone from the middle of the bus had the courage to stand up and say, "Excuse me, where are you going?"

The stoic man didn't respond, he looked straight ahead, waiting for the ramp to deploy and then wheeled out onto the highway. Shortly after, others rose from their seats. What began as a few quickly turned into the entire group of eighty people shuffling out of their seats and rushing down the aisle toward the exit.

The large group spilled out onto the empty highway and were met with the brisk air. Many didn't even have the proper attire to endure the elements for any long period of time.

"Now what are we supposed to do?" someone asked.

In situations such as these, it's natural to look for a leader. The paraplegic man didn't exactly fit the bill physically, but he at least seemed to know more about the situation than the others. He therefore become the default leader. The group formed a semi-circle around him, asking him a barrage of questions like a pack of desperate news reporters.

"Do you know why we were abducted and put on this bus?" someone asked.

"I want to know where the bus was taking us."

"I'm hungry."

"I'm cold."

The paraplegic man had yet to respond. Just then, he spoke, which silenced the huddled mass, "I wish I could give you the answers in which you all seek, but I'm afraid time is of the essence."

"Time is of the essence for what?"

"Are we in danger?"

"You tell me?" the man said. "You were all taken against your wills, bound by your hands and feet, and placed on a bus, being transported somewhere without your consent. Were you provide any information as to why you were taken or where you are going? To me, this strongly suggests that we're all in grave danger and therefore it would be in our best interest to run and hide."

"Do you know who's behind this?" someone from the crowd asked.

"Wait, where are you going?" another person asked.

They all watched as the man rose from his chair and began to walk with the assistance of a mechanical contraption affixed to his body.

"Is that an exoskeleton?" Dane asked a question that did not receive a response.

"I think it's best we split up into smaller groups," the man said. "Anyone who wants to join me is welcome to come."

Eight people immediately stepped forward from the crowd, leaving the others standing around looking at each other.

"Hey, I'm Dane. What's yours?"

"You can call me Mr. Camouflage."

"Mr. Camouflage?" Dane repeated. "I'm definitely not going to call you that. How about Camo, or Cam?"

"I don't know what's going on, but I don't want to get into any more trouble," someone said. "I'm just going to wait here."

"Yeah, me too."

"I'm with you. I don't want to go into the forest. I don't even know what I'm supposed to be running from."

The crowd started to chat amongst themselves and form groups based on shared sentiments. Some opted to remain on the driver-less bus where it was warm while others decided to head off on their own.

"You can't stay here," Mr. Camouflage insisted to those heading back onto the bus. "They'll be here soon, and if they find you, they will kill you."

"Who?"

"There's no time to explain, you just have to trust me. Our best chance for survival is to split up into smaller groups and hide."

From the distance, the headlights of what appeared to be one oncoming vehicle sped toward the group. Upon closer inspection, there were two other large vans trailing behind. The small convoy of vehicles approached hastily and came to a stop. The vans were slower, but eventually caught up and pulled into position.

A dozen armed men in full combat gear exited the vehicles and surrounded the bus. Establishing a perimeter, several men entered the bus with their guns raised high. There were a handful of people who had rejected Mr. Camouflage's warning and remained behind.

"Who are you?" one of the old ladies on the bus asked.

Without hesitation, one of the men aimed his weapon and shot her in the head, killing her instantly. A hailstorm of gunshots could be heard in the distance. Each gunshot echoed throughout the forest, sending bone-chilling shivers up the spines of the group. They knew each blast meant one of their former bus mates was being killed. Dane and his small crew stopped momentarily, but were encouraged to continue.

"What the hell is going on?" Dane demanded. "Were those gunshots?"

"Yes, but we need to keep moving or else we're going to be next," Cam insisted, trudging through the dense forest. "It'll be dark soon, we need to get as far away from here as possible."

"I don't know if I can carry on," someone from the group said.

"Fine, stay here and die, but I strongly suggest we stick together," Mr. Camo said.

"I think I'm having a panic attack," Dane said. "I can't breathe."

"Look, Dane," a man in the group said. "I want to know what the hell is going on just as badly as you do, okay? But right now, I much rather live another day and see my son.

There'll be a time and a place to ask questions. For now, I suggest we listen to this gentlemen over here and keep moving."

Dane let out a huff before setting off again to catch up with the rest of the pack.

The heightened anxiety gave them all a boost of adrenaline, which helped push their bodies to their limits and continue on for as long as possible.

Making their way through the forest and uneven terrain wasn't easy to begin with. Now with the sun setting lower on the horizon, less light penetrated the dense trees making it increasingly more difficult to see. A night chill set in, testing their resolve and inducing even more of a panic state. The naïve ones of the group were quickly realizing that they would sleep outside in the cold unforgiving night.

"Hey, Mr. Camouflage," a pretty woman said, gasping for breath. "I need to stop."

"Yeah, I'm with her," another one from the group said. "I'm not sure how much further I can go on. We've been on the move for several hours and I'm pretty sure my feet are covered in blisters."

The group came to an agreement to settle in for the night before the sun completely set. They found a clearing amongst the trees, which appeared to be as good a spot as any.

One of the men from the group took charge and said, "Can you two gather as many little sticks as you can find?" He then turned to two ladies. "We need to find long, slender sticks, preferably without any branches."

Dane took inventory of the group. "Hey, wait, we're missing someone," he said, looking around. "There was nine of us. Who's missing?"

"The girl," one of the group members said. "The quiet girl."

"What was her name?"

"She didn't say."

"She hasn't said anything."

"Has anybody seen her?"

"I remember seeing her about an hour ago," someone said.

"She's probably just using the bathroom."

"Do you think she got lost?"

"If she did, there's no way we're going to find her. I suggest we make camp and let her find us."

"Maybe it's a good idea going forward for each of us to have a buddy. We'll be responsible for that buddy at all times. There's eight of us, so it works perfectly."

They took a minute to find partners and introduce themselves. It was the first chance they had to do that since being on the bus.

Dane partnered up with a towering man with large muscles who introduced himself as Train, an obvious nickname. The two complemented each other nicely since Dane was lean and not as physically gifted. He made up for that by being quick-witted and creative, two undervalued qualities in a survival situation.

"What do you want me to do?" Dane asked, happy to follow orders.

"I need you to help me start a fire," Train said. "First, we need large stones to make a fire pit. Then we need to gather kindle and firewood."

Each pair was delegated a specific task and everyone worked diligently to set up camp before it became completely dark.

"So tell me... how did you get the name Train?"

"I got it from my football days. I was a linebacker?"

"I don't know what that means."

"It means I was a protector."

"I guess I picked a good buddy then, huh?"

"Yes, you did," Train said with a chuckle.

Train was a bit hard to read. Standing over 6'5" with hulking muscles, he was certainly an intimidating looking man, but so far he seemed kind and gentle.

As they worked alongside one another, Dane took notice of the tribal tattoos covering Train's skin. Among them appeared to be several military markings common for soldiers who had endured combat.

"You fight in the war?" Dane asked.

"Of course, who didn't?"

"Well… I didn't. I'm not much of a fighter. I'm an artist. I'm more of the creative type. I'd rather write a poem about war than be in a war, if you know what I mean."

"War makes us all fighters."

"Not me, it turned me into a coward."

"How can you call yourself a coward? Where I come from, no man would ever speak those words."

"I'm not much of a man apparently, and I'm okay with that. What do you do… I mean, when you're not fighting and looking for firewood?"

"I do various things. It's hard to put a label on me."

"I hear ya, brother. You mentioned you son, what's his name?"

"Caleb."

"How old is Caleb?"

"He's ten."

"What is that, fifth grade?"

"Fourth."

"Oh nice."

"You have any kids?"

"Uh… sort of, not really."

"What does that mean?"

"It's complicated."

"Baby mama drama?"

"Exactly."

They both shared a laugh.

Carrying large stones back to camp, Dane plopped them down on the ground and began arranging them in a circle. He was sweaty and exhausted, but wanted to do his part to contribute.

Just before nightfall, the missing group member appeared from the darkness without saying a word. She didn't seem pleased to see everyone, nor did she attempt to make friends. Instead she kept to herself, sitting by the fire to stay warm.

"Hey, the quiet girl is back," Dane announced. "Where were you?"

"I got lost," she said.

"Well, we're glad to have you back," an older lady said with a welcoming smile. "We came up with the idea of having a buddy system while you were away. Since there are now nine of us, you can be in a group with us. I'm Cheryl, what's your name?"

"Allie."

"It's nice to meet you, Allie."

"Perhaps we should all properly introduce ourselves," Dane suggested. "We can tell everyone a bit about our backgrounds, what we do for a living, our education, and skills. It'll help us get to know each other, but also give us an understanding of our unique strengths and what we can offer to the group. I can go first."

Everyone shuffled into position and took seats around the fire. They didn't have any food, water, or shelter, but they were at least warm. And they had each other.

"So as many of you know, I'm Dane. I told you a bit about what I do for work. I'm recently single, I live alone. I would say my strengths are intelligence and creativity. I'm an ideas guy. I pride myself on being an outside-of-the-box thinker so I'm sure that will come in handy at some point."

When Dane was finished, the person sitting to his left went next.

"I'm Cheryl, I'm a former lawyer, former mayor… former a lot of things actually. Before the war I was the mayor of a small county, but now that county is… well, you can probably guess. I'm one of the few survivors and I feel very fortunate about that. Currently, I'm in between roles, still trying to figure out what the next stage of my career and life are going to be."

"What are your strengths?" Dane asked.

"I'd say leadership, policy, law… I'm very organized. I'm not sure what use any of those are in this environment, but I'm happy to help in any way I can."

"That's great, thank you for sharing, Cheryl," Dane said.

"I'm Lynn, I was a surgeon, but a year ago I was involved in a devastating automobile accident which claimed the life of my husband and crushed both of my hands. After a long and difficult recovery, I was no longer able to perform surgery. Despite that, I still have vast amounts of knowledge of the human body."

"I'm sure your skills will come in very handy with first aid and other ailments we may encounter. It's nice to meet you, Lynn."

After listening to some of the stories, a thread stood out, but Dane waited until he heard from everyone to confirm his hypothesis.

"I'm Lauren… Lauren Larkin, some of you may recognize me. I was a former model and humanitarian. My strengths are being headstrong, standing up for what I believe, fighting for what's right, and ensuring everyone is treated equally and fairly."

"Thank you, Lauren," Dane said with a smile. "It's nice to have you in the group. Okay, who's next? Train, would you like to go?"

"My name is Train," he said stoically, in a deep and soothing voice.

"Is there anything else you'd like to share with the group?" Cheryl asked.

"No."

"Very well, then. Who's next?"

"I can go next, a soft spoken Mexican man said. My name is Mauricio. I'm a construction worker. I'm good with my hands, I can fix just about anything. I can fight."

"Perfect, we're glad to have you, Mauricio."

They had made it through nearly half the group and so far people were being fairly reserved. They were reluctant to open up and share too much personal details. Some weren't even comfortable giving their real name.

Going around the campfire, an older man who had an eccentric look was next in line.

"I don't know about the rest of you, but I'm starving," he said.

"Ah, don't mention food," Lauren said.

"I thought models were used to starving themselves," Dane said.

Lauren shot him an evil look.

"What's your name, where are you from?" Cheryl ask an elderly man to her right.

"You can call me Professor," the man said. "I'm a scientist, an inventor, and a mathematician. I hold two PhDs, several patents, and a long list of inventions."

There was an arrogance about the Professor that was off-putting. He spoke in a demeaning way as if the rest of the group weren't on his level intellectually. Everyone could hardly wait for his turn to be over.

As the introductions went around the campfire, there was one person everyone was eager to hear from. He was mysterious and seemed to know more than anyone about the situation they were in. With eager ears, everyone turned to him.

"I go by the name Mr. Camouflage," the man said, "but if that's too long for you to say, you can call me Cam, or Camo. As you can see, I'm a paraplegic. I lost the use of my legs in… an accident. I'm good with computers, and…. um, well… that's pretty much it."

"Can you please tell us what you know about why we're all here?" Cheryl said.

After a brief pause, the man said, "Yes, I think the time has come for you all to know the truth."

www.ingramcontent.com/pod-product-compliance
Lightning Source LLC
Chambersburg PA
CBHW032222050726
47591CB00001B/225